sew zoey

sewing in circles

written by
Chloe Taylor

illustrated by
Nancy Zhang

Simon Spotlight
New York London Toronto Sydney New Delhi

This book is a work of fiction. Any references to historical events, real people, or real places are used fictitiously. Other names, characters, places, and events are products of the author's imagination, and any resemblance to actual events or places or persons, living or dead, is entirely coincidental.

SIMON SPOTLIGHT
An imprint of Simon & Schuster Children's Publishing Division
1230 Avenue of the Americas, New York, New York 10020
First Simon Spotlight hardcover edition September 2015
Copyright © 2015 by Simon and Schuster, Inc.
All rights reserved, including the right of reproduction in whole or in part in any form.
SIMON SPOTLIGHT and colophon are registered trademarks of Simon & Schuster, Inc.
For information about special discounts for bulk purchases, please contact Simon & Schuster Special Sales at 1-866-506-1949 or business@simonandschuster.com.
Text by Sarah Darer Littman
Designed by Laura Roode
Manufactured in the United States of America 0815 FFG
10 9 8 7 6 5 4 3 2 1
ISBN 978-1-4814-4033-2 (hc)
ISBN 978-1-4814-4032-5 (pbk)
ISBN 978-1-4814-4034-9 (eBook)
Library of Congress Catalog Card Number 2014959226

CHAPTER 1

Hearts for a Sweetheart

Exciting news! There's going to be a new member of the family—a baby cousin. Aunt Lulu and Uncle John don't know yet if it's going to be a boy—or a girl. Or if they do, they're not telling—so I designed a unisex onesie that will work either way. Baby clothes are so cute, don't you think? It's hard to believe that right this minute, inside Aunt Lulu's bump, there's a tiny little person growing who is going to be wearing them someday. It's hard to believe Marcus and I were once newborns, but Dad's got the pictures to prove it. We spent a fun, but bittersweet, night looking at our baby albums.

Marcus is so lucky because he actually *remembers* things about Mom. Me, I only know her through what other people have told me. The one thing pretty much everyone's told me is that I've inherited her creativity for making clothes. What's the sewing equivalent of a "chip off the old block"?

"Hey, Zoey, do you think these buttons would look cute as decorations for a little cross-body purse?"

Zoey Webber and Allie Lovallo—a fellow fashion blogger who until recently had dated Zoey's older brother, Marcus—were browsing at their favorite store, A Stitch in Time. Even though they'd been friends before Allie and Marcus had started dating, the fact that Allie was seeing someone else and had hurt Marcus so much caused a rift in their friend-ship, one that Allie was trying to mend by regularly inviting Zoey to hang out.

"Those are cute, but maybe a little big?" Zoey said. "I'd be afraid they might catch on a door handle and break or something. What about these instead?"

She pointed to some iridescent purple and blue glass buttons.

"Good point," Allie said. "And those are fab."

She took a few sets and put them in her shop-ping basket.

Zoey found small heart-shaped buttons she was thinking of using for the baby outfit she was mak-ing for her cousin-to-be.

"Those are adorable!" Allie exclaimed. "You're going to have so much fun making things for your new cousin."

"I know," Zoey said, grabbing plastic snaps and zippers. "I went to Peek-a-Boo to get some ideas, and everything there was just soooooo cute and teensy, like little doll's clothes."

The two girls went to the cash register to pay

Jan, the owner of A Stitch in Time, for their fashion finds.

"I like your choices," Jan said. "And of course, my favorite young designers get the special up-and-comer discount."

"Thanks, Jan!" Zoey said. Jan's discounts really helped her get more for her money.

"Thanks, Jan," Allie echoed. "Hey, Zoey, can I buy you a hot chocolate with the money I just saved?"

"Sounds yummy!" Zoey said. "But, Allie, you don't have to do that. . . ."

Allie paused. "I want to."

"Whatever you do, enjoy!" Jan called after them as they waved good-bye. "And get extra whipped cream."

At the nearby coffee shop, Allie and Zoey settled into two plush chairs near the front window with their mugs of hot chocolate. The girls chatted about fashions they'd seen in the latest issue of *Très Chic*, which they'd both received in the mail the previous day.

During a lull in the conversation, Allie picked at a loose thread on the chair's upholstery.

"So . . . have you ever thought about getting a booth at the Mapleton gift fair?" she asked as Zoey took a cautious sip from her still-steaming mug. "I did it last year, and it was really fun." Allie blew on her hot chocolate to cool it. "I also sold a lot of stuff. Maybe you should apply for a booth this year!"

Zoey considered the idea. It wasn't something she'd ever thought of doing, but now that Allie mentioned it, she could see the possibilities.

"It would be kind of cool to sell directly to people for a change," she said. Zoey had only ever sold her clothing online and to friends and neighbors— never in an actual store.

"It's also a great way to get customer feedback," Allie said. "Even when people don't buy things, you get to see which items they pick up and look at the most."

Zoey placed her hot chocolate on the table as she got to the question that was really worrying her about the idea. "Is it expensive to rent a booth?" she asked.

"You can pick a booth size that fits your budget when you fill out the application," Allie replied. She went on to explain that the organizers of the gift fair asked applicants to send pictures of their work, and they tried not to accept too many vendors with the same kind of merchandise. It was a carefully curated gift fair.

"Do you think I'd have a chance with a Sew Zoey booth?" Zoey asked.

"Yes! You should apply!" Allie said. "It would be fun to do the fair together."

"I'll definitely think about it," Zoey said.

"Great," Allie said. She looked down at her phone and smiled. Something about the look on her face made Zoey think it was about Oliver, the boy Allie had started seeing when she'd broken up with Marcus.

"Are you still seeing that guy?" Zoey asked.

Allie blushed and put away her phone. "Yes, we're still going out."

Zoey decided to change the subject back to the safer topic of clothes. They spent the rest of the time talking about their current design projects.

Zoey enjoyed being able to talk to someone who understood fashion the way Allie did—so much that she was able to relax and almost forget that Allie had ever dated her brother and hurt his feelings by breaking up with him. Well, at least until Allie pulled into the driveway to drop her back home.

"So . . . how's Marcus doing these days?" Allie asked.

There was an awkward silence as Zoey tried to figure out what she should or shouldn't say. She wished they could agree to not discuss her brother if they were going to stay friends.

"He's okay," Zoey said finally. "You know, he's . . . moving on."

"That's good to hear," Allie said.

Zoey really didn't want to talk about her brother with his ex-girlfriend. She'd spent enough time playing an uncomfortable intermediary between the two of them.

"Well, gotta go," Zoey said, opening the car door to get out.

"It was good to hang out again," Allie called

after her. "And don't forget to think about the gift fair!"

"I won't!" Zoey promised, and shut the door.

As Allie drove off, Zoey wondered how long it would take before things were 100 percent back to normal between them. She hoped it was sooner rather than later. Being in friendship limbo was really awkward.

Marcus was in the kitchen snacking on peanut butter and an apple when Zoey walked in.

"Was that Allie's car?" he asked.

"Yeah," Zoey said, hoping he wouldn't ask any uncomfortable questions. "She wants me to apply for a booth at the gift fair."

"Did she ask about me?"

"She asked how you were." Zoey sighed.

"What did you say?"

"I said you were moving on," Zoey said.

"And what did she say?" Marcus asked.

"She said 'good,' or something like that," Zoey said.

"That's all?"

Marcus looked disappointed that Allie hadn't

been more interested in the topic of, well, him.

"Yeah, that's all," Zoey said. "I'm going upstairs."

"Hey, Zo?"

Zoey stopped in the doorway and then turned back to face her brother.

"I'm glad you guys are hanging out again despite . . . you know, everything," he said. "I know Allie's one of the few people who understands what it's like to be a fashion whiz."

Zoey breathed a sigh of relief.

"I'm glad too," she said. "I missed talking to her."

"I just want you to know I'm okay with it," Marcus said. "At least, I'm trying really hard to be all mature and grown-up and everything."

"Thanks, Marcus," Zoey said. "I appreciate it. I really do!"

"Enough to let me eat the last brownie, even though I've already had three?" Marcus asked with a hopeful grin.

"Wow, that's a tough call," Zoey said. But then she smiled. "Yeah, go ahead. I'm full from the hot chocolate, anyway!"

During lunch in school the next day, Zoey floated the idea of the gift fair to her friends.

"What do you think?" she asked. "I like the idea, but I'm worried about all the money I'd have to lay out in advance for the booth. What happens if I don't sell enough to cover it?"

"I think it's a fashiontastic idea! It'll be like a real clothing store!" Priti Holbrooke said. "Why haven't you done something like this before?"

"She's sold her clothes on Etsy," Kate Mackey pointed out.

"And Allie and I did the pop-up store on Etsy, too," Zoey said.

"But this would be the first time people could see your clothes in person," Priti countered.

The girls considered this as they ate their lunches.

"I guess that's true. Shopping's more fun when you can really see what you're getting," Libby Flynn said. "*Especially* when it comes to clothes."

"But what if I don't make back the money I have to pay for the booth?" Zoey worried. "Also, I'm jumping the gun. You have to apply to be selected."

"You took a risk with Doggie Duds, and that worked out," Kate reminded her.

Zoey thought back on all the risky projects she'd attempted in the last year or so. They certainly hadn't been without their nail-biting moments, but they'd always turned out okay in the end.

"Why wouldn't they select you for the gift fair?" Priti argued. "You've been on *Fashion Showdown*! Bryn Allen was on the cover of *Celebrity* magazine, wearing one of your designs. I mean, you're practically . . . *world famous!*"

Zoey burst out laughing.

"Stop, Priti! You're making me blush!" she said. "I'm hardly world famous."

Zoey reached into her backpack. "Speaking of gift fairs, I've got some gifts for you guys."

She handed each of her friends unique versions of the fabric bracelet she'd previously copied for Ivy Wallace when Emily Gooding was nagging Ivy to buy one. The bracelets were all the rage after having been featured in a recent issue of *Très Chic* magazine.

Libby's was made of two different fabrics—one

printed with little candies and the other with little carrots—to remind her of how hard she'd worked for the local food pantry for her Bat Mitzvah project. Kate's fabric was covered in daisies, because those were her favorite flowers. Zoey figured a flowery bracelet was a subtle way for Kate to bring florals into her look. And Zoey had made Priti's bracelet with a fabric printed with stars, to signify her friend's love of being in the spotlight.

"Wow!" Libby said. "I love it! I've been wanting one of these bracelets ever since I saw them in *Très Chic!*"

"These are just like the ones Emily brags about all the time," Kate, who was more into reading about sports than fashion, said.

"I love mine!" Priti said. "It's so me!"

"I'm touched you remembered daisies are my favorite flowers, Zoey," Kate said. "But . . . why did you buy us presents when it's not anyone's birthday?"

"I didn't buy them," Zoey explained. "I made them."

Priti and Libby stared at her, shocked.

"I knew I hadn't seen these fabric patterns before, but I thought you had some kind of special connection or something," Libby said. "Like, maybe you got them before the general public could."

"No," Zoey said. "I just made them myself, inspired by the ones in *Très Chic* and, well, everywhere."

"Are you allowed to do that?" Priti asked.

"Why not?" Zoey said.

Priti shrugged. "I don't know. Never mind." She put on her bracelet and held out her arm. "I love the design, though."

"Oh! Now I get the design on mine," Libby said. "It's about my mitzvah project, right?"

"That's right!" Zoey said. "The candy is for the sweets theme, and the carrots are because you grew vegetables and raised the money for the new fridge for the food pantry."

"That's so cool!" Libby said. "Although I have to admit that I'm glad my Bat Mitzvah is over—well, except for writing all the thank-you notes. That's taking *forever*."

"You must have hundreds to write," Priti said.

"I haven't counted, but it's a lot!" Libby said. "I'm pacing myself. I try to do a few every night and then some on the weekends, when I'm not volunteering at the food pantry, just so I can get them over with." She looked over at Kate. "That reminds me . . . I haven't seen you and Tyler at the food pantry lately."

"That's because we're not going out anymore," Kate said.

"Wait, what?!" Priti exclaimed. "When did that happen? And why?"

"We decided about a week ago," Kate said.

"And you didn't tell us?" Priti said.

Kate shrugged.

"But why did you break up?" Zoey asked.

"Don't get me wrong—Tyler's a nice guy and all. But it's not like we spent that much time together," Kate explained. "And then we fought at Libby's Bat Mitzvah—"

"But you worked that out, didn't you?" Zoey said.

"Kind of," Kate said. "But in the end, we realized we were better off as friends." She looked around the table at the other girls' concerned faces. "It's the best thing. Really."

"Are you sure?" Libby asked. "You guys seemed to have fun together at the food pantry."

"We can still have fun, but as friends," Kate said. She smiled. "I'm okay with it. Really, I am."

Kate's smile was genuine, but Zoey couldn't help wondering if her friend seemed just a little . . . *too* okay. She resolved to investigate further.

CHAPTER 2

Spot the Gifts

I'm thinking of doing a gift fair for the first time. Allie suggested it—she's the one who I did the Accessories from A to Z pop-up store with on Etsy. She's done it before and said it was worthwhile. You have to apply to get in. I'm worried about whether I'll get chosen, but even more worried about whether I'll make back the money I'll have to pay to rent the booth. What do you think? Have any of you ever done a gift fair before? How'd it go?

My friends think it's a good idea. I mean, who doesn't like getting clothes as gifts? Well, I guess if you get something boring, like socks or a tie, it could be kind of a letdown—but I wouldn't sell those at my booth! I've designed these items because they're cute and easy to make in different sizes. I hope it'll be enough to display in a booth in an interesting and decorative way. Doing an Etsy store was so much easier! But it'll be good experience to meet my customers face-to-face, right? I sure hope so.

Zoey stood outside Mapleton Prep after school on Wednesday, waiting for Allie to pick her up. Allie had printed out the applications for the gift fair, and they were going to Poppa's Pastry Shop to work on them together, since Allie'd already taken part last year and knew what she was doing.

"Not taking the bus today, Zoey?" Ms. Austen,

the school principal, asked as she walked up to Zoey.

Zoey really liked Ms. Austen. Not only was she a great principal, but she also had a fabulous sense of style and really cared about Zoey and the other students.

"No, my friend Allie is picking me up," Zoey said. "She's going to help me apply for a booth at the Mapleton Gift Fair."

"That's a great gift fair!" Ms. Austen said. "I went last year and bought presents for my family." Her brow wrinkled. "I don't remember seeing that many clothing booths, though. It was mostly gifts and accessories."

"Oh," Zoey said, crestfallen. "Hmm. I wonder if maybe it's just not a clothes kind of fair."

"Not at all!" Ms. Austen said. "I probably just don't remember seeing the clothes, because I wasn't looking for them. Also, I like to try things on before I buy them, and that's the problem with a gift fair—there's no dressing room."

"I never thought of that," Zoey admitted.

Allie's car pulled into the parking lot.

Ms. Austen put her hand on Zoey's shoulder.

"Don't let me discourage you, Zoey. I'm sure your things would do really well. Your designs have that special something."

"Thanks, Ms. Austen," Zoey said, smiling as she opened Allie's car door. "See you tomorrow!"

Ms. Austen waved as they drove away.

"So, Zoey," Allie said as they walked into Poppa's Pastry Shop. "Are you ready for some exciting paperwork?"

"Um . . ."

"Well, how about hot chocolate and not-so-exciting paperwork?" Allie amended.

"That sounds more like it," Zoey said.

After getting their drinks, they found a big empty table, so they could spread out, and Allie got the applications out of her bag.

"Okay, so first you have to figure out what size booth you want, because they're all different prices," Allie said.

"I don't know," Zoey said. "What size did you get last year?"

"I got the smallest one, but I'm selling accessories,

which are small. You're selling clothes, which need more room to be displayed properly."

"Oh. Yeah. I didn't even think about that," Zoey said.

"What I did last year was sketch out a design of how I thought I wanted my booth to look, and that made it easier to figure out how big it should be," Allie said. "Like, first figure out what you think you're going to want to sell there, then how you'd display it to attract customers."

Zoey pulled out her sketchbook and pencils from her backpack. She had to determine which pieces she wanted to sell. She didn't want to choose too many items, because she'd have to make each one in a range of sizes.

Allie was busy filling in her application, but Zoey picked out a few design sketches to show her.

"What do you think of these for the gift fair?"

"I like the short-sleeve sweatshirt and the skirt," Allie said. "Also, that dress is cute."

"I picked things that are pretty easy to make," Zoey said.

"Smart," Allie said. "If you want, I can help you

figure out what size booth you need. But don't forget, you have to rent the display racks and tables and stuff, too."

It wasn't just more complicated than Zoey thought. It was starting to sound more expensive, too. Zoey worried as she started working on the layout of her display.

When she had the basic idea down on paper, she showed it to Allie.

"That looks good," Allie said. "Okay, every booth has a table, but you'll need racks and something to display a sign—maybe a stand? And some of the shelves and clothing rods that hook onto the walls of the booth—I'd get some extra of those since you have clothes. . . ."

Allie went down the list of display items and insisted that Zoey order a variety of options.

"But it's going to add up to so much money!" Zoey complained. "What if I don't make it back?"

"I'm pretty sure you will," Allie said. "It's a really popular market. And in any event, it'll give you really good exposure for your stuff. But if you skimp on materials and people can't see your pieces, they won't sell. Trust me. It's worth it."

"I guess," Zoey said, but she still worried about the cost.

Allie helped her figure out the expenses for the order form. Zoey swallowed, hard, when she saw the total. It was even more than she'd thought it would be.

"Now, all you have left to do is take pictures of the products and figure out the pricing," Allie said. "The gift fair organizers want to make sure that the vendors fit in with their aesthetic, and also that they have gifts available at different price ranges, so that everyone who comes can find something they can afford."

"Okay," Zoey said. "I'll get Marcus to take the pictures when I get home, and with Dad's and Aunt Lulu's help, I'll decide on prices."

"Make sure you mail it tomorrow," Allie warned her. "The deadline is Friday."

"I will," Zoey promised.

"One other thing: They don't give you a lot of time between when they tell you you're accepted and when the gift fair opens. Last year, I had to scramble to get all my stuff made on time," Allie said, "so I'd start making stuff even before you find out if you're accepted. Especially since I'm sure you will be, anyway."

"Thanks," Zoey said.

Zoey was still excited about the gift fair idea— but after Allie dropped her back at the house, Zoey stared at the total cost again. It was a lot of money to lay out for the booth and display supplies rental. Zoey figured maybe Allie was being a little overly cautious by suggesting that she order so many supplies. Zoey crossed out a few things here and there and recalculated the total. It seemed more manageable, although the number still made her gulp.

Marcus was in his room, listening to music while he did his homework. Luckily, the music seemed more upbeat than it had been since Allie had broken up with him. Maybe he really *was* moving on. Zoey knocked on his door and walked in.

"Hey, Marcus—can you take pictures of some of my pieces on Marie Antoinette?" Zoey asked, referring to her headless dressmaker's dummy. "I'm applying for a booth at a gift fair, and they want to see my work."

"Sure," her brother said. He got up and grabbed his camera. "So you decided to do it?"

"Well, I'm applying," Zoey said as they walked into her room. "Allie seems pretty sure I'll get in, which means I need to start making stuff right away."

Marcus laughed as he set up the shot to take a picture of a T-shirt on Marie Antoinette. "You mean you're not going to be in a crazy last-minute Zoey panic like you usually are?"

"No, I'm trying to break the habit," Zoey said. "I'm going to start tonight and try to make a few pieces every day, so I don't have to do a marathon sewing session right before the fair."

"Good plan," Marcus said. "Okay, what's next?"

Zoey took the T-shirt off the dummy and slid a simple shift dress over her dress form.

"I've chosen my most versatile and flattering pieces," she said. "And new ones that are easy to sew, because I'm going to have to make them all in small, medium, and large sizes."

"I hate to ask, but what happens if you don't get chosen and you've made all the sizes?" Marcus asked, taking a picture of the dress.

"I'm going to think positively," Zoey said. "And if worst comes to worst, I can always try to sell them online on my Etsy store, right?"

"Sounds like you've thought of everything," Marcus said.

"I sure hope so!" Zoey said.

After putting the application in the mailbox, there wasn't much else Zoey could do—other than get started making clothes—while she waited to see if she'd been accepted. But she gave herself a break from sewing for the rest of the day. She had something—or rather, someone—else on her mind.

"So how is your friend Ezra Marks from Hebrew school?" she asked Libby as casually as she could at the school the next day.

"Fine," Libby said. She smiled. "Funny, he asked me how you were doing, too."

"He did?" Zoey exclaimed. "You didn't tell me that!"

"You didn't tell me either," Priti grumbled. "That's *important news*, Libby!"

"Okay, okay! *Sorry!*" Libby said. "He said he really enjoyed hanging out with you at the Bat Mitzvah."

"I really enjoyed hanging out with him, too," Zoey admitted. "He's nice—and cute, too."

"He *does* seem fun," Kate said. "But not my type."

"I just had an idea!" Libby said. "I'll invite a bunch of people over to my house on Saturday—and one of those people can just *happen* to be Ezra!"

"Won't that look too obvious?" Zoey asked, even though she was excited about the thought of seeing Ezra again.

"Why would it look obvious?" Kate said. "As long as Ezra's not the only one Libby invites from her Hebrew school."

"Which he won't be," Libby said.

"Perfect!" Priti exclaimed. "Let Operation Cupid commence!"

Zoey alternated between being nervous and excited for the rest of the week. Luckily, she was trying to keep to her self-imposed schedule for making gift fair items, and that kept her from constantly dwelling on the get-together at Libby's. But still . . . She had to figure out what to wear.

She ended up being late leaving for Libby's house, because she tried on five different outfits and the same amount of hairstyles before finally deciding on a braided bun, and a cropped hot-pink sweater with bobbles on it, layered over a tank top. She was also wearing patterned jeans she'd bought with her aunt Lulu at a consignment shop.

"How do I look?" she asked her dad when she got into the car, where he'd been waiting patiently while Zoey did a last-minute change of her shoes.

"Cute!" Dad said. "I like whatever you did with your hair."

He pulled out of the driveway.

"Do I look cute . . . or pretty?" Zoey asked.

Mr. Webber looked at her, bemused. "Why do I have this awful feeling that whatever answer I give you is going to be the wrong one?" he said. "Both?"

Zoey sighed.

"I just want to look good tonight," she said.

"You always look great, Zo," Dad said.

"You have to say that. You're my dad."

"But I mean it," her father said. "I'm not just saying it because I'm your dad." He glanced over at her. "Is there any special reason you want to look nice?"

Zoey blushed. "No reason," she said, looking out the window.

Dad chuckled. "No reason you want to share with your dad, at least," he said.

"Can we stop talking about this?" Zoey said.

"Sure!" Dad said. "So, how about that ball game this afternoon?"

When they got to Libby's house, Zoey rang the doorbell and then waved good-bye to her dad.

"Ezra's here," Libby told Zoey in a low voice when she answered the door. "And he asked if you'd arrived yet."

"Well, I'm here now," Zoey whispered. "I had a major case of fashion indecisiveness!"

"I love what you came up with!" Libby said. "Come on, join the party."

Everyone was hanging out in the family room,

which was the biggest room in the house. Priti and Kate were playing a dance video game with some of Libby's Hebrew school friends they'd met at the Bat Mitzvah. Zoey saw Ezra sitting on the sofa, looking at his phone, but he looked up and smiled as soon as he noticed her standing there.

"Hey, Zoey, how's it going?" he called out. "Making lots of new clothes?"

"I am," Zoey said. She walked to the sofa, and Ezra moved over to make room for her to sit next to him. "I'm applying for a booth at the Mapleton Gift Fair. I'm busy making pieces I plan to sell, if I get chosen, that is."

"That's really cool," Ezra said. "Good luck. It must be hard to wait for them to decide."

"I've been trying not to think about it too much," Zoey confessed.

"I'm sure they'll choose you," Ezra said. "I checked out your blog. Your designs are really good."

Ezra checked out my blog? Zoey thought.

"I didn't think a fashion blog would be up your alley," she joked.

Zoey could have sworn Ezra's cheeks were red

when she saw him pick at a nonexistent thread on his jeans.

"I guess . . . I was curious. I thought it was cool that you make clothes," he admitted.

Now, Zoey felt her own cheeks starting to flush.

"I really liked your sketches, too," Ezra continued. "I draw—and paint."

"You do?" Zoey asked. "What kind of paintings?"

"Different things—landscapes. A few still lifes. Some abstracts. I'm still finding my style."

He pulled out his phone and showed her a photo. "Here's one of my latest landscapes."

Ezra has a great eye for color, Zoey thought.

"Wow, that's really good," she said.

"Do you think so?" Ezra asked. "You're not just saying that?"

Zoey chuckled, because he sounded just like she did when she was asking her dad how she looked on the way to Libby's house.

"No, I'm not," she said. "I promise."

Ezra smiled, and Zoey thought he looked even cuter, if that were possible.

"I was thinking . . . ," he said. "My parents

are taking me to the state fair next weekend. Do you . . . maybe . . . want to come with me? Well, with us, since it's my whole family going."

Zoey wanted to get up and dance. *Ezra was asking her out on a date!*

But instead, she stayed sitting on the couch, and said, "Sure! Well, as long as my dad says it's okay."

"Great!" Ezra exclaimed. "It should be fun."

They smiled at each other, and then Ezra said, "So, do you want to challenge Priti and Kate in a dance-off? They seem like the reigning champs."

"They're good, but I bet we can beat them," Zoey said.

Ezra stood up and held out his hand to Zoey.

"Come on, Zoey. Let's dance!"

"What do you wear on a date to the state fair with your date's parents, carnival rides that are wardrobe malfunctions waiting to happen, and lots of delicious fried food?" Zoey asked her friends at lunch on Monday. "I'm so nervous!"

"Aren't you excited?" Libby said.

"Oh, definitely!" Zoey said. "But I've never been

on a date. I still can't believe a guy I like actually likes me back!"

"Of course he likes you," Priti said. "You're fabulous!"

Her friends all laughed, nodding in agreement.

"Just relax and be yourself," Kate said. "Think of it as hanging out, rather than as a date. That's what I've done the few times I've gone on dates."

"Thanks," Zoey said. "I'll try to remember to do that. But . . . you guys still haven't helped me answer the all-important outfit question!"

"Something comfortable," Kate said. "And a top that won't flip up on a ride."

"And cute," Priti added. "But parent friendly, so not too low-cut."

"Maybe a denim skirt?" Libby suggested. "Or cute overalls?"

"Good idea!" Zoey said. "With a chambray shirt or something like that. Or maybe gingham? Sounds a little costumey, but I'll try to make it feel more modern."

"I knew you'd think of something," Priti said.

"Well, that's because I have such good friends

to help me," Zoey said, smiling at the girls sitting around the table. "Otherwise, I'd still be panicking!"

"You and Ezra seemed to be having a lot of fun at Libby's house on Saturday night," Kate said to Zoey on the bus ride home that afternoon. "I wouldn't worry too much about going to the state fair with him. I bet you're going to have a really good time."

Kate had more experience on the dating front than Zoey did—but she'd just broken up with Tyler, for reasons Zoey didn't entirely understand.

"I know," Zoey said. "Kate . . . I hope you don't mind my asking, but . . . can you explain more about why you broke up with Tyler? It just seems kind of . . . sudden."

"Oh . . . well, it's no big deal, really. It's just . . . when we talked more about the fight we had at Libby's Bat Mitzvah, I realized that Tyler was always noticing how Libby dressed—and just noticing Libby, period. I was worried it might create tension between her and me," Kate said. "I mean, I like Tyler a lot, but Libby's one of my very best friends, and the last thing I want do is compete with my best friend for some guy's attention, right?"

"That *would* be really awkward—for everyone," Zoey said.

"So I figured that even though I liked him, it wasn't worth risking the potential drama," Kate said.

"I can see that," Zoey said. "I guess I've just been confused, because you seem so unfazed by breaking up. Like it doesn't upset you at all."

"Oh . . . yeah. About that . . . I didn't want Libby to find out why we broke up, because I was afraid she'd think it was her fault. So I've been trying to play it cool," Kate said. "But to tell you the truth, it hasn't been that bad." She fiddled with the fastening on her backpack. "In fact, I've been feeling kind of guilty that I *haven't* felt more upset."

"You shouldn't feel guilty," Zoey told her. "That's probably a sign that it just wasn't meant to be."

Kate gave a relieved smile. "Maybe you're right," she said.

"It's too bad things got weird with you two," Zoey said. "Tyler seemed like a nice guy."

"He *is* a nice guy," Kate said. "But I guess . . . Well, part of what I liked about him was that he seemed to want to get to know the real me. But then once we started going out, he kept suggesting that I change my style to become more girly—even if, like he said, it was just because he liked the way Libby dressed, not because he wanted me to be more like Libby. But still . . . it felt like he was trying to change me—and I didn't like it."

"Of course not!" Zoey exclaimed. "You should never change for anyone, unless it feels right for you and it's something you really want to do. Okay, lecture's over."

"Right now, I'm happy to just be me, without a boyfriend," Kate admitted. "I'm looking forward to having to think about just school and sports!"

CHAPTER 3

Looking Fairly Fabulous

Yee-haw! I'm going to the state fair with a friend and his family. I've never been, but the theme of the fair is "Udderly Amazing!," so I figured there are going to be cows and other farm animals there. Dad went to the state fair when he was younger, and he said that it's not just farm animals and tractors—there are fair rides, too. He also said I should bring a good appetite, because there's every kind of fried food you could possibly imagine—even *fried Oreos*! I can't wait! ☺

"Okay, kids—I've leaving you money so you can order in. I've got a date tonight," Dad said, putting down some crisp bills onto the kitchen counter.

"Is it with the same person?" Zoey asked. She noticed her father was wearing aftershave, and the shirt she'd helped him choose a few months ago when they went to New York to meet Daphne Shaw, Zoey's favorite designer and fashion fairy godmother, at her design studio.

Dad blushed and then started wiping nonexistent crumbs off the counter. "Yes, it is," he said.

"Are we ever going to meet her?" Marcus asked.

"Of course," Dad said. "I just don't want to rush things."

Marcus glanced at Zoey. "*Rush things?* You've been out on plenty of dates already," he said. "It's hardly *rushing* things."

"Soon, Marcus," Dad said. "Just . . . be a little patient, okay?"

"Okay, but I don't understand the secrecy, that's all," Marcus complained.

"All in good time, I promise," Dad said. "I've got to run. Don't want to be late! See you later."

As soon as the door closed behind him, Marcus exploded. "It's so silly," he exclaimed. "Why won't he introduce us to this Mystery Lady?"

"He seems shy about her," Zoey said. "Or maybe *she's* shy."

"But they've been dating for a while," Marcus argued. "And it's not like we're that scary. Okay, maybe *you* are, but I'm not."

"Ha-ha, very funny," Zoey said. "To tell you the truth, I'm not even sure I *want* to meet her now. Between Priti's parents getting divorced, and you and Allie breaking up, and now Kate and Tyler not being together, I don't think I can handle any more relationship drama in my life. Especially when it's grown-up, affecting-me-personally drama."

"But . . . she seems to make Dad so *happy*," Marcus observed.

Thinking about it, Zoey realized that Marcus had a point. Since Dad had been dating the Mystery Lady, he was more cheerful, smiling when he thought no one was watching. He certainly seemed to be paying more attention to what he was wearing!

"I think this is the real deal," Marcus continued. "And just in case Dad is worried we'd be freaked out about him being involved with someone other than Mom, we should tell him we'll be fine with him being in a serious relationship that makes him happy."

"I guess," Zoey said.

But deep down, she wondered if she *was* okay with it. Of course, she wanted her dad to be happy. But was she ready for a stepmom?

As was her habit, as soon as she'd finished her after-school snack, Zoey checked her blog and her e-mail. One name stood out in her in-box—DAPHNE SHAW!

Dear Zoey,
I hope school—and all your exciting sewing

projects—are going well. I've got a proposition for you that I hope you'll find exciting, too!

I'm doing a pop-up store at a major department store in New York City—and this one will have a tween focus—inspired by *you*! I've had so much fun making pieces for you and your friend Libby, so this is a way to test the idea of a new Daphne Shaw tween line in a limited way.

The department store is already onboard—especially after the success they had with Cecily Chen's tween line not long ago. Since you and Sew Zoey are my inspiration, I had this great idea, and I hope you like it: I'd love to feature one of your pieces in the pop-up shop. What better place to spotlight an actual tween designer's work than in a designer's tween fashion line pop-up shop?

What do you think? If you're interested, I'd need you to express mail me a box with a few sample pieces you can produce in multiple sizes, right away (I'll give our account number to your dad so he can arrange the shipping)—so I can select which one will work best alongside my own collection. I hope you are as excited about this as I am! ☺

Let me know!

Daphne

Zoey had to read the e-mail twice before she believed it. It was too good to be true—except after reading the e-mail for a third time, just to be extra especially sure, Zoey knew it was!

She e-mailed Daphne back right away and said that she was definitely interested, and she'd get together the pieces to send to her as soon as possible.

The news made it hard to concentrate on doing homework, because she kept imagining seeing one of her designs on display in a New York department store!

After finally finishing her work, she paged through her sketchbook, trying to figure out which designs might work. Nothing seemed quite special enough to be next to Daphne's own designs.

"Marcus! Zoey! Dinner's on the table!" Dad called from downstairs.

Zoey had been so involved in her design deliberations, she hadn't even realized she was hungry. But now that Dad said dinner was on the table, she heard the growls coming from her stomach.

She headed down to the kitchen, where her father was removing a delicious-smelling lasagna from the oven.

"Yum," Zoey said. "That smells awesome. Did you make it?"

"No, I bought it at Paola's," Dad said. "I had a busy day."

"Paola's lasagna?" Marcus said, walking into the kitchen and slouching into a chair. "Sweet!"

After they all had served themselves generous portions and tasted a few scrumptious bites, Zoey told her father and Marcus about Daphne's exciting e-mail.

"I know I've said this before, Zo, but you are so fortunate to have a mentor like Daphne Shaw," Dad said. "This sounds like an incredible opportunity."

Marcus nodded and gave Zoey a pointed look. "Speaking of opportunities . . ." he said. "Zoey? Is this a good time?"

Zoey knew he was trying to say he wanted to ask their dad about the Mystery Lady, but she wasn't ready to do it. She glared back at Marcus.

"Uh, kids? What's going on?" Dad asked. "You've obviously got something on your minds. Are you trying to plan some kind of surprise?"

"Not exactly," Zoey said. "It's more like you are."

Dad looked even more puzzled.

"I am?" he said. "That's news to me."

Zoey looked over at Marcus and gave him a *C'mon, it's your turn!* look.

But Marcus seemed to be having second thoughts, too. Maybe he was remembering how private their dad was about his dating life—except for when he occasionally asked Zoey for fashion advice.

Dad looked from Marcus to Zoey and back to Marcus. "Okay, kids," he said. "Spit it out. What's on your minds?"

Zoey looked down at her lap. This whole thing was Marcus's idea. No way was *she* going to be the one to speak up!

"Well, Dad . . . The thing is . . . Zoey and I are both mature. . . . Well, *I* am, and Zoey kind of is. . . ."

"I'm just as mature as you are!" Zoey protested.

"Let's stipulate that you're both mature," Dad said to head off any argument. "So . . ."

"So, we think it's time we meet this person you're spending so much time with," Marcus said. "I mean, we're mature enough to know she might not be The One, or whatever, but it just seems strange you've been seeing her so much without introducing us."

Zoey expected Dad to say, "Sure, I'll invite her over this weekend!" but to her surprise, his brow furrowed and he looked nervous.

"I don't know," he said. "I'm not sure if she's ready to meet you guys yet."

"We promise we won't bite," Zoey said.

Dad laughed. "She knows that," he said. "And I promise to talk to her about meeting you, okay?"

"Okay," Zoey said.

But Marcus wasn't so easily satisfied. "When you say she isn't ready to meet us, is that because she doesn't like that you have kids?" he asked. "Or that she doesn't like kids at all?"

Zoey hadn't even thought of that. She couldn't

imagine her dad going out with anyone who didn't like kids!

Dad burst out laughing.

"Marcus, I promise you—nothing could be further from the truth," he said. "Once you meet her, you'll understand." Suddenly more serious, he said, "I'll talk to her. It'll be as soon as she feels comfortable doing it. Hopefully, it won't be too long now."

Zoey wondered how long "too long now" would be. Marcus apparently wondered the same thing, because after dinner he came into her room and sat on the end of her bed.

"Wasn't that the weirdest convo with Dad we've ever had?" he asked.

"If it wasn't the weirdest, it was definitely a contender for weirdest," Zoey agreed.

"He's being so cryptic about the Mystery Lady," Marcus complained. "'Once you meet her, you'll understand.'"

"I know, right?" Zoey exclaimed. "But then he won't say *when* we get to meet her!"

"Which only makes me want to meet her even more," Marcus said.

"Maybe that's the plan!" Zoey said. Then she thought about it. "No, that's not Dad's style."

"No, definitely not Dad's style," Marcus agreed.

"I'm more curious about her than ever," Zoey said. "*Soon* can't come soon enough!"

"You'll never guess what happened!" Zoey told Priti in industrial arts the next day.

"Should I try, or are you just going to tell me?" Priti asked.

"I'll just tell you because it's too awesome to make you guess," Zoey said. "Daphne Shaw is doing a pop-up store in a Manhattan department store for a new tween line, and she wants to feature one of my pieces, since I was one of her inspirations!" Zoey gasped for air after rattling off her good news in one breath.

"For real?" Priti exclaimed.

"Yep!" Zoey said, a big grin lighting her face. "But I can hardly believe it!"

"That is so awesome!" Priti said. "Do you, like, get to go to the opening and be photographed by paparazzi and all that stuff?"

"I don't know," Zoey said. "I hadn't even thought about that kind of thing. I was just excited that she asked me to be part of it!"

Ivy, who'd overhead Zoey telling Priti, smiled in an unexpectedly friendly way. "Zoey, that's really amazing. I'm happy for you," Ivy told her.

Even though Ivy had been nicer to her since the reversal in her family fortunes, Zoey was still surprised that Ivy seemed genuinely pleased to hear of her good news.

"Thanks, Ivy. I'm really excited."

"When does the pop-up shop open?" Ivy asked.

"I'm not sure," Zoey said. "I just have to get Daphne some samples quickly, so she can decide which design will work best with her collection."

"Good luck!" Ivy said, before walking away to go use the table saw.

Priti elbowed Zoey. "What's got into Ivy all of a sudden? Why is she being nice to you?"

Zoey hesitated. She'd promised Ivy that she wouldn't tell anyone about seeing her and her mom picking up supplies at the food pantry, because Ivy's father had lost his job and they'd been struggling financially. But how else could she explain to Priti why Ivy had suddenly developed some compassion for others?

"I don't know," she said. "People change, I guess."

Priti gave her a sideways look.

"We're talking about *Ivy Wallace*, your supreme nemesis!" she said. "I don't trust this sudden transformation into Nice Ivy. Be careful, that's all I'm saying."

Zoey wasn't sure she trusted it either, but knowing what she knew, she felt like she wanted to give Ivy the benefit of the doubt.

"I will," she promised Priti. "I will."

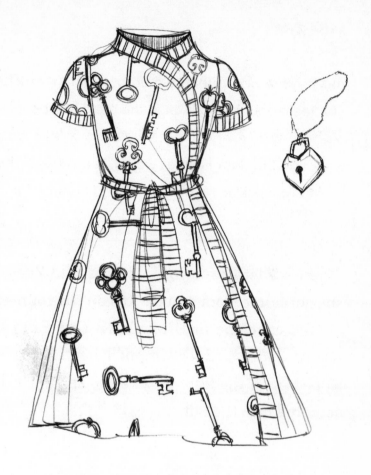

---------- CHAPTER 4 ----------

Lock and Key

I've got some potentially very exciting news that I can't share yet—but keep your fingers crossed. Sorry to have to keep it under lock and key—the inspiration for today's designs—but I don't want to jinx anything. Mine's not the only mystery around here. I can't tell you much more about that, either, but I know exactly how you feel about being kept in the dark! Maybe if I wasn't so busy with everything else, I'd do a little detective work, like Sherlock Holmes would. I could wear this cute dress and necklace as I went around hunting for clues.

"There's a letter for you," Marcus told Zoey when she got home from school. "It's on the counter."

The envelope had "Mapleton Gift Fair" as the return address. Zoey dropped her backpack and ripped open the letter, excited to see if she'd been accepted into the fair.

Dear Ms. Webber,

Thank you for your application to the Mapleton Gift Fair. While we found your designs charming, we haven't had the greatest success with clothing vendors in the past, because of the lack of dressing room facilities and because clothes are harder to buy as gifts than other items. Therefore, we've made the decision to cut back on clothing vendors and are sorry we cannot offer you a booth at this year's gift fair.

Sincerely,

Mapleton Gift Fair Planning Committee

Zoey's heart sank. She'd been counting on getting a booth. Allie had made it sound like it was almost a sure thing. Plus, she'd already told Ezra about it, and he'd been so excited for her. Now, she was going to have to tell him that it wasn't happening after all. That would teach her to jinx things by talking about them before they were a done deal!

Maybe she should have submitted accessories instead of clothes, Zoey thought. Except that would have put her directly in competition with Allie, and that didn't seem right given that Allie was the one who recommended she apply for a booth. It wouldn't be very considerate. But then Allie hadn't been especially considerate of her feelings lately, had she?

Zoey sighed.

"What's the matter?" Marcus asked. "You're looking pretty glum all of a sudden."

"I didn't get accepted for the gift fair." Zoey sighed again.

"What!" Marcus exclaimed. "Why not?"

"They're cutting back on clothing vendors, because clothes don't sell as well as other items," Zoey said.

"That stinks," Marcus said. "Haven't you made a whole bunch of stuff for the fair already?"

"I have." Zoey sighed a third time. "And now it's all going to go to waste, unless . . . Wait! I know!"

Marcus stared at her, taking in the sudden transformation of her face from discouraged to cheerful.

"Why do I sense that you've had a sudden brainstorm?" he said.

"Because I have!" Zoey laughed. "I found the silver lining. Since I already like the pieces I made for the gift fair, and they're relatively simple to make in different sizes, they'll be perfect for Daphne Shaw's pop-up shop. Can you drive me to FedEx? I just need a few minutes to pack a box to send."

"If it helps turn your frown upside down, sure!" Marcus said. "Hey, by the way, did you see the other thing that came in the mail?"

"What?" Zoey asked.

"We got the invitation to Aunt Lulu's baby shower. And it's addressed to you, me, Dad, and 'guest.'"

"Wow—so . . . do you think the Mystery Lady is going to come?" Zoey asked. "Will we finally get to meet her?"

"That's what I plan to ask Dad tonight," Marcus said.

When they posed the baby shower question to their father over dinner, he looked distinctly uncomfortable.

"Look, kids, I talked to her about meeting you,

and she's just not ready," Dad said. "So she's not coming to the baby shower."

Marcus looked mutinous. "I just don't get it, Dad. What does she have against us?"

"I promise you, she has nothing against you," Dad said. "You'll understand when you meet her, I promise."

But Zoey and Marcus weren't so easily convinced. After dinner, Marcus joined Zoey in her room to complain about the situation.

"I'm starting to think there's something weird about this lady," he said. "Why else would she be so afraid of meeting us?"

"I know! We're not *that* scary," Zoey said. "Well, maybe you are, but *I'm* not!"

"I'm not sure I want things to work out between them anymore," Marcus said. "I'm worried that she's strange or cold or something."

"Me too," Zoey said. "Except . . . Dad still seems really happy every time he gets back from a date with her. So . . . there's that."

Marcus sighed. "Yeah, there's that. And it's a pretty big that."

"I guess we have to be patient, like Dad says," Zoey said.

"True," Marcus agreed. "But that doesn't mean we have to like it!"

Later that evening, Aunt Lulu called to speak to Zoey.

"Did you get the invitation to the baby shower?" her aunt asked.

"Yes," Zoey said. "It's really cute."

"Zo, I need your help. I've been looking for a simple, but cute, outfit to wear for the shower, but everything I've seen and tried on so far just makes me look big and dowdy," Aunt Lulu complained. "Can you rescue me from mom-to-be madness and design me something stylish?"

"I guess . . . ," Zoey said. "I mean, I'll try. It's just . . . I have no idea how to make maternity clothes. I'm not sure how much room I'm supposed to leave for the bump."

"I don't want you to stress about it," Aunt Lulu said. "I'll buy another dress as backup, just in case. But I love your designs, and I trust you to create something that won't make me feel frumpy."

"I can't imagine you ever looking frumpy!" Zoey told her aunt. "You always look fashionable to me."

Aunt Lulu laughed.

"Just another reason why I love you, Zo," she said. "I guess I just feel frumpy because I'm not used to having a bump!"

"Don't worry, Aunt Lulu," Zoey said. "I'll make you something that you will feel good wearing . . . or at least I'll try."

"I know," Aunt Lulu said. "I'm sure I'll love whatever you make."

Saturday dawned crisp and cool, with a sunny blue sky—perfect weather for a visit to the state fair on a date. Zoey put on her overalls-minidress and gingham shirt and a pair of comfortable sneakers, because Ezra warned her there would be a *lot* of walking!

"Are you looking forward to your rustic adventure?" Dad asked. "You look prepared . . . and lovely."

"I think so," Zoey said, smiling at her dad's compliment.

"Make sure you have some fried Oreos," Marcus said. "They're awesome."

"*Everything* tastes good fried," Dad said. "The problem is it's not healthy!"

"*Everything?*" Zoey asked. "Even . . . broccoli rabe? It's so bitter!"

"I bet if I put on a thick coating of breading and deep fried some broccoli rabe, even Zoey would eat them," Dad said.

Marcus laughed. "Now, *that* I'd like to see!"

"Blegh," Zoey said, sticking out her tongue. "No, thanks."

Just then the doorbell rang.

"Sounds like your date is here," Dad said.

"Be normal. Don't be embarrassing," Zoey said.

"*Embarrassing?* Who, us?" Marcus joked.

Zoey glared at him as she went to open the door for Ezra.

"Hi, Zoey!" he said, looking really cute in a gingham shirt, and jeans. Then he noticed her outfit and grinned. "Great taste in shirts!"

Zoey laughed. "Yeah, we kind of look like the Farm Twins, don't we?"

"I like your outfit," Ezra said. "So, are you ready to rock the fair?"

"Definitely," Zoey said. She turned and saw Dad and Marcus standing in the kitchen doorway, waiting for their introductions.

"Ezra, meet my dad and Marcus," she blurted out quickly. "Okay, time to go!"

"Nice to meet you, Mr. Webber," Ezra said. "And Marcus."

"And you, too, Ezra, however briefly," Zoey's dad replied, grinning as Zoey hurried out the door.

"I apologize in advance for anything embarrassing that my parents or siblings do today," Ezra said as they walked to his car. "I begged them to be on their best behavior, but there are no guarantees."

Zoey laughed.

"I told my dad and brother to 'be normal' when you rang the doorbell," she said.

"Well, they did a good job," Ezra said, smiling. "I hope my family does as well!"

Ezra's younger brother, Robbie, and sister, Amelia, were cute and very talkative. Ezra and Zoey kept them busy playing I Spy and word games, which made the ride to the state fair pass quickly. Ezra's parents were nice, too—he'd obviously told them about Zoey's and her blog, and they asked her questions about her designs.

"Ezra said you're going to have a booth at the Mapleton Gift Fair this year," Mrs. Marks said. "That's a great event. I go every year."

"Oh . . . ," Zoey said. "Well . . . actually . . . I didn't get selected. They're cutting back on clothing vendors this year."

"That's too bad," Mrs. Marks said.

"Better luck next year," Ezra said.

"I hope so." Zoey sighed.

When they arrived at the fair, Mr. and Mrs. Marks checked that Zoey and Ezra had their cell phones and arranged a meeting time and place for later. Then they took the younger kids off to see the sights and left Zoey and Ezra to their own devices.

"What do you want to do first?" Ezra asked. "That sign says we can milk cows. Wanna try?"

"Sure!" Zoey said. "I've only ever got milk from a carton!"

They watched a video on how to milk a cow,

and then they got to try on a real-live cow.

It turned out milking a cow was harder than it looked.

"I never realized that milk is warm when it comes out," Ezra said, sitting on the milking stool, his face against the cow's side. "Although if you think about it, it makes sense!"

"We're used to drinking milk cold out of the fridge," Zoey said, struggling to eke a dribble of milk from the cow's udder into the bucket below. "This looked a lot easier in the video!"

After realizing they weren't going to make it as milkmaids, they moved on to try to guess the weight of the enormous butter sculpture of a cow, a butter churn, and a round of cheese.

The prize was a year's supply of . . . butter!

"Do they just give you the sculpture as the prize?" Zoey asked as she filled in her blank entry.

"I hope not!" Ezra said. "It must get pretty dirty after everyone looking at it and sneezing and everything!"

"True," Zoey said. "Yuck! If I win, I definitely want fresh, clean, unsneezed-on butter!"

After visiting the sheep and the goats, Zoey and Ezra decided it was time to go on some rides. They hit the flying swings, the tilt-a-whirl, and finally the giant Ferris wheel. When their car reached the top of the wheel, they took in the view, and Ezra reached for Zoey's hand.

Zoey wondered if he was going to kiss her. She half wanted him to and was half nervous about it. But he didn't. They just sat and looked out over the fair.

"You don't realize how big this place is until you see it from up here," Ezra said.

"I know!" Zoey agreed. "There's a huge farm machinery section we haven't even visited."

"You don't have a room for a tractor in your garage," Ezra said.

"True," Zoey said. "But I think I'm making room for some fried Oreos in my stomach. Marcus said they were amazing."

"As soon as we get back on the ground, we'll investigate the fried everything aisle!" Ezra promised.

And they did. Zoey tried fried zucchini, fried

okra, fried macaroni-and-cheese balls, fried dough, a variety of fried desserts, and finally fried Oreos, which were just as amazing as her brother had promised.

"I'm so full, I don't think I can walk," Zoey groaned after licking the last of the Oreos from her fingers.

"I know how you feel," Ezra said. "Good thing it's time to go meet my parents!"

"Can you believe they have fried cotton candy?" Zoey said.

"If you can eat it, we will fry it! I think that's the official motto of every state fair." Ezra laughed.

"And if it's not, it should be," Zoey agreed. She smiled at Ezra. "Thanks for a really fun day."

CHAPTER 5

Room to Grow

How fast do babies grow? I hope I've left enough room for my new cousin in the dress I've designed for Aunt Lulu to wear at the baby shower. I'm not exactly an expert in the maternity field. The only experience I've had with growing things is with plants, and I don't think they're quite the same as human babies when it comes to growth rates!

I had a great time at the state fair. Fried Oreos are delicious. So are fried macaroni-and-cheese balls, fried Twinkies, fried Snickers bars, fried cotton candy, and even fried okra! If all vegetables were fried, maybe I'd even eat the ones I don't like.

My outfit managed to survive without any wardrobe malfunctions on the rides, and it turned out that my friend also likes gingham shirts, so we matched!

"I know it's only Tuesday, but I still haven't heard anything back from Daphne," Zoey complained to her dad and Marcus at dinner.

"Wait . . . didn't I just drive you to FedEx to send her the box on Friday?" Marcus asked.

"Well, yeah," Zoey admitted.

"And like you say, it's only Tuesday," Marcus pointed out. "Give your poor fashion fairy god-mother a break!"

"Yes, but—"

"She's a very busy lady, Zo," Dad said. "And

this has happened before, remember? You were all stressed out because you hadn't heard from Daphne, and it turned out she was out of the country visiting fabric manufacturers in China."

"I know." Zoey sighed. "This just feels . . . different somehow. And I want to be in her pop-up shop *so badly!*"

"Don't worry," Dad told her. "I'm sure Daphne will come through, just like she always does."

Even though she tried not to think about it constantly, Zoey wasn't very successful. Not only that, she checked her e-mail at every possible opportunity, to see if Daphne had sent anything yet. Finally, on Thursday she checked her phone at lunchtime, and saw an e-mail from Daphne Shaw in her in-box.

"Daphne finally wrote!" she exclaimed, opening the e-mail to read to her friends.

"'Dear Zoey,'" she read. "'Thank you for being so wonderfully prompt with the samples. I'm sorry to say that I—'"

Zoey faded into silence as her eyes scanned the end of the sentence. It wasn't good news.

"Don't leave us in suspense!" Priti said. "She's sorry to say *what*?"

Zoey stared blankly at a spot of spilled milk in the center of the table.

"She's sorry to say that she wasn't taken by any of the pieces I sent—they aren't up to my 'usual level of creative innovation.'"

"Ouch," Libby winced.

"Oh, Zoey . . . ," Kate said.

Zoey tried to hide how crushed she felt, but it wasn't easy. She never thought she'd get a rejection like that from her mentor. Not from Daphne.

"It's not the end of the world," she said, attempting to convince herself more than anyone else. "She gave me an idea of what she's looking for, and she's letting me submit a few more designs."

"Well, that's good!" Priti said. "She's giving you a second chance."

"But what if my second chance isn't good enough?" Zoey worried. "Can you imagine how awful it'll be with Ivy? She heard me telling you about the pop-up shop, and now if Daphne doesn't like any of my designs, she'll think I was lying! And even though she's been nicer to me lately, I bet that'll be all it'll take to get on her bad side again."

"You can't live your life worrying about what Ivy's going to think," Libby said. "Or what she's going to do."

"And why shouldn't your second chance be good enough?" Kate asked. "Daphne's loved all your work before."

"I don't know." Zoey sighed. "I just can't believe that both things I was looking forward to so much have fallen through—the gift fair and now Daphne's pop-up shop. From now on, I'm not going to talk about anything exciting until it actually happens!"

That evening, after telling her dad and brother about the disappointing news, Zoey went to her bedroom to work on new ideas. She sat at her work-table, pencil in hand, trying to come up with some fresh clothing designs for the pop-up shop, based on Daphne's guidance. Normally, she had so many ideas, it was hard to get them out of her head and onto the paper fast enough. But with her confidence rattled, every time she started to sketch, she second guessed herself. *What if it turns out awful? What if it's not up to my usual level of creative innovation? What if I'm just not good enough?*

She heard the phone ring but was busy worrying, so she let Marcus get it.

"Zo! It's for you!" he shouted.

When she picked up, the woman on the other end introduced herself as Mrs. Perry and said she was one of the organizers of the gift fair.

"We've had a cancellation, and we'd like to offer you a booth, if you're still interested," she said. "Are you?"

Finally! Some good news! Zoey thought.

"Yes! I am!" she exclaimed.

"Oh good," Mrs. Perry said. "There's just one caveat: We'd like you to add more accessories to your offerings, because they're easier to sell as gifts. Would you be willing to do that?"

"Sure," Zoey said—although as soon as she agreed, she wondered if it would cause problems with Allie.

"Great!" Mrs. Perry said. "We'll see you on setup day!"

Zoey thought for a few moments after hanging up the phone, then she dialed Allie's number.

"Hey, Allie—good news! I got a booth!"

"You did? That's awesome!"

"Yeah, there was a cancellation," Zoey explained. "I was wondering—could we get together tomorrow to talk details?"

"Sure!" Allie said. "I'll come over at . . . How does ten sound?"

"Sounds good," Zoey said.

Hopefully, Marcus would sleep late, so she wouldn't have to deal with any awkwardness between her brother and his former girlfriend. And hopefully, she'd be able to talk through the accessories situation with Allie.

Mr. Webber was reading the paper and drinking coffee in the kitchen when Allie arrived the next morning.

"Allie Lovallo! Nice to see you," he said. "It's been a while."

Zoey flashed her father an *Oh, Dad!* look. Did he have to make a point about the fact she hadn't been around as much . . . *for obvious and awkward reasons*?

"Great to see you, too, Mr. Webber," Allie said.

"Let's go in the living room," Zoey said. "So we can talk."

"I've got pictures of some new belts I'm going to be selling at the gift fair," Allie said. "I can't wait to show you."

The girls sat on the sofa, and Allie took out her phone and started swiping through photos of her newest accessories.

"What do you think?" she asked Zoey.

"They're fab," Zoey said. "I like the one with the beads."

"Yeah, that's my favorite, too," Allie said. "I like it so much, I almost don't want to sell it!"

"Speaking of selling . . . um . . . One of the conditions of me getting the booth at the gift fair is that I have to offer more accessories," Zoey said.

"Oh," Allie said.

"Are you upset?" Zoey asked.

"No, not upset," Allie said. "I totally understand. I just don't want to feel like it's some kind of competition, because we're both going to be selling accessories."

"I don't think it will be," Zoey said. "I mean, our styles are different enough that there's room for both of us, don't you think?"

"Yeah," Allie said. "That's true."

"How about we just promise not to let it get weird?" Zoey suggested.

"Sounds like a plan," Allie agreed. "I'm up for a No Weirdness Pact."

Once they'd shaken on it, Zoey felt better about the whole thing, although secretly she wondered if they'd actually be able to keep to their weird-free pledge.

"Hey, Zo—Oh . . . Allie." Marcus stood in the doorway in his pajamas, his hair standing up every which way.

"Hi, Marcus," Allie said, standing up as if the sofa had suddenly caught fire. "I was just leaving."

Zoey looked at her, surprised. Allie hadn't said anything about leaving until Marcus walked in the room. Zoey wondered if the awkwardness between her friend and her brother would ever end.

"Don't leave on my account," Marcus said. "I'm going to get something to eat."

"No, it's okay," Allie said. "I've got a bunch of stuff to get done today with the gift fair coming up so soon."

"How are . . . things?" Marcus asked.

"Good!" Allie said brightly. "Busy!"

She picked up her bag and car keys.

"See you soon, Zoey! I'm glad you're in the show!"

"Yeah, me too," Zoey said, although right now, she was feeling pretty awkward about everything to be too glad about it!

Zoey spent Sunday trying to come up with ideas for accessories that would be different enough from Allie's merchandise that it wouldn't seem like they were competing. She kept coming back to the fabric bracelets—like the ones she'd made for Ivy and for her friends. They were pretty easy to make, they looked great, and they were really popular.

She sketched out several new designs to add to the ones that had been popular at school. The more she thought about it, the more she was convinced that the bracelets were the best solution.

The following day, she showed the new designs to her friends and explained the latest about the gift fair situation.

"I want to stay away from earrings and necklaces, so I'm not directly competing with Allie," she continued.

Zoey noticed that Priti didn't seem as excited and enthusiastic about her designs as usual.

"What's the matter?" she asked.

"Well, it just seems a little . . . I don't know . . . hypocritical, is all," Priti said. "I mean, when my cousin's friend in India copied the sari you made me to wear to my cousin's wedding and sold the knock-offs in her clothing store, you freaked out because she was copying your work and making a profit."

She leaned forward, as if to emphasize her point.

"But now you're doing exactly the same thing with these bracelets," Priti said. "Copying someone else's design to make a profit. I don't want to get into a fight like we did last time, but I don't understand why one is okay and the other isn't."

Zoey was taken aback—and, truth be told, upset—by her friend's criticism.

"I'm not a hypocrite!" she protested.

"I don't want to make things weird again," Priti said, clearly distressed. "I just want to understand why there's a difference."

"I can see Priti's point," Kate said, ever the diplomat.

"Me too," Libby said. "But I also love the bracelets Zoey made for us, so maybe I'm a hypocrite too."

"I mean . . . well, when I got upset before, it was early on," Zoey explained. "And now I've learned from being in the fashion business for a while that people make copies all the time. It's just the way it is, and Daphne Shaw told me to accept it as a compliment when people copy my designs."

"I guess that makes sense," Priti said. "Now I understand better."

"It would be different if I were claiming these were the authentic bracelets and charging the full price," Zoey said. "But the ones I make are my interpretation of the popular design, and I would be selling them at a lower price."

"That's true," Libby said.

"I like yours better, anyway," Kate said.

"I'll try to think of something else to make and sell at the fair," Zoey said, feeling unsure of what to do. "I just have to figure out whatever it is in a hurry, because there isn't much time left! Plus, I still have to send more pieces to Daphne Shaw, but I'm stumped about how to design something that shows off my creativity or whatever. I thought *anything* I made was creative."

"I wonder if the clothes for the fair were too basic, since you meant them to be crowd-pleasers, you know? She probably just wants to see your personality in the clothes for her shop," Priti said, then got an idea. "What if you pull the pieces from your closet that feel the most like you, the ones that are *so* Zoey?"

While Priti laughed at her own pun, Zoey hugged her. "Thank you, you're brilliant!" Zoey finally said, breathing a sigh of relief. "I couldn't wrap my head around what Daphne might be looking for, but I think you're on to something. And if I choose the pieces I really love, it means they fit well and have appeal. I know just the pieces I'm going to pick and mail!"

"See, it'll work out," Libby said.

That night, after scouring her closet for Daphne-worthy designs, Zoey decided on a few pieces to give to her dad to mail in the morning. Dad and Marcus were watching a ball game in the living room when she came downstairs with the clothes, so she waited until she saw that it was a commercial break before she got their attention.

Zoey said she'd made a decision for the second round of ideas for Daphne's shop and showed them her choices.

"You're sending your favorite skirt?" her dad asked.

"How will you live without it?" Marcus added. "It's practically your uniform."

Zoey cringed at the thought of uniforms. "Well, I decided to send things that were both creative and wearable, and most of all, very me. These are things

I usually want to wear, so hopefully, Daphne will think other people will want to wear—and buy—them too," Zoey said. "Besides, I guess it wouldn't hurt for me to give the skirt a break in my clothing rotation."

"That's my girl!" Dad said. "I'll pack and mail these first thing in the morning."

Dad and Marcus gave Zoey high fives, and then the game came back on, so Zoey headed over to her work area. She was relieved to have found pieces she could really feel good about sending to Daphne—pieces that represented her as a designer and a person. To get a head start, in case Daphne liked one of them, Zoey had made patterns based on the pieces she'd sent, and got to work cutting out fabric in a variety of clothing sizes.

When she needed a break from that, she switched gears and focused on the gift fair dilemma. She looked at all the accessories she'd made in the past, trying to figure out if maybe she could use them instead of the bracelets for the gift fair. Some were much more complicated and time-consuming to make than the bracelets, and others were about the same, but she didn't think they'd sell as well. She still had to make a few more clothing items in different sizes for the gift fair. Even though she liked the clothes, she was a bit worried they might not be good enough for the fair, since they weren't good enough for Daphne. The truth was, she just didn't have time to sew new outfits, and deep down, she liked what she had made, anyway. So she decided to focus on the accessories.

Do I let quick and easy win over any niggling worries I have about copying the bracelets? she wondered.

She was going to have to make a decision—and soon.

CHAPTER 6

Switchbacks and Roundabouts

Have you ever been on one of those roads going up a mountain where there are lots of switchbacks or hairpin turns? Sometimes they're even called "dead man's curves," but that freaks me out! It can make you kind of dizzy. But also, it's exciting, like you're on a roller coaster. That's what it's been like around here lately—and it inspired the roundabout shirt and tote bag. I get excited, then go around a corner and get disappointed, then get excited again, then hit another bend. . . . I hope the road ahead gets a lot straighter and less complicated soon!

"What are you making?" Priti asked Zoey in industrial arts the next day.

Zoey was on the lathe, chiseling a piece of wood into a cylinder.

"I'm trying to make wooden beads," Zoey said. "I was thinking that if I can make enough of them, I could do wooden bracelets for the gift fair."

She stopped the lathe.

"But at the rate I'm going, there's no way that's going to happen. It's taking waaaaay too long to make the beads, let alone varnishing them and making them into bracelets."

"They do look pretty fiddly," Priti admitted.

"That's it. I'm giving up on the bead idea." Zoey sighed. "Time to turn to plan B. I think I'm going to make some wooden trays instead. They'll be good for displaying things, and I can even sell them. They're kind of accessories, right?"

"Those will definitely be easier to make," Priti said. "And they'll look good in your booth."

Zoey took the wood cylinder off the lathe and went to find some wood to make a tray. As she was looking through the woodpile for a suitable piece, she overheard Emily asking Ivy about the bracelet Zoey had made her. Ivy had been wearing it constantly.

"Where did you get that cool bracelet?" Emily asked. "I've never seen that pattern before—and I know pretty much all the ones they make."

"Oh, it was a gift from a . . . friend," Ivy said. "Isn't it great?"

Emily took a closer look. "Wait—let me see the clasp. . . . That's not the same kind as mine. And it doesn't have the charm with the brand logo," she said. "That bracelet is a fake. I guess whoever gave it to you as a present isn't *that* good of a friend after all."

Zoey glanced at Ivy, who looked mortified.

"It's real. I'm sure it is," Ivy said. "But I don't really like it that much, anyway."

She tore the bracelet from her wrist and shoved it into her backpack. When Ivy looked up, she caught Zoey's eye and gave her an angry look.

Zoey felt terrible. She'd only made Ivy the bracelet because Emily had been harassing Ivy about when she was going to buy one, and after seeing Ivy at the food pantry and learning the secret about her dad losing his job, Zoey had wanted to try to make Ivy's life easier. Now her kind gesture seemed to have backfired.

I have to find a way to talk to Ivy after class and explain, Zoey thought. She didn't know Ivy had thought the bracelet was store bought or that it would matter so much that it wasn't.

Finding Ivy wasn't so easy. It seemed like she was trying to avoid Zoey. It wasn't until the next day that Zoey finally spotted her going into the girls' room and followed her. All the stall doors were open, except one.

"Ivy?" Zoey called through the door. "It's Zoey."

"What do *you* want?" Ivy said, sounding even angrier than Zoey expected.

"I need to talk to you," Zoey said. "About the bracelet. It's okay, we're alone."

The toilet flushed, and Ivy came out and went to the sink.

She gave Zoey a dirty look in the mirror. "Oh, you mean the *fake* bracelet? The one you made to humiliate me in front of Emily?"

"I didn't, I—"

"Do you know I purposely learned everyone's schedule at the food pantry, so I could make sure we never go to pick up food when Libby, Kate, or Tyler is there?" Ivy said, ripping paper towels out of the dispenser angrily and drying her hands. "And now you had to do this."

"Ivy, I promise you, I would never do anything to embarrass you on purpose," Zoey told her. "I was only trying to be nice!"

Ivy threw the paper towels into the garbage. "Yeah? How do you figure that?"

"Well . . . because in industrial arts, I kept hearing Emily asking you when you were going to buy a bracelet, and you kept on making excuses about why you hadn't bought one yet," Zoey explained. "And then when I saw you and your mom at the food pantry, and you told me about your dad losing his job, I realized *why* you hadn't bought one."

"You haven't told anyone, have you?" Ivy demanded.

"Of course not!" Zoey said. "I wouldn't do that! I just wanted to help you in some way, so since I like crafts and stuff, I figured I could make you a bracelet to try to get Emily off your back. I guess I should have bought one instead, but I didn't realize it was so important to you to have the real thing."

Ivy gave her a skeptical look.

"I don't get it. Why would you want to be nice to me after how I treated you?" she asked.

Only Ivy would assume the worst about someone being kind, Zoey thought.

"You've been nicer to me lately," Zoey explained. "And . . . I just figured everyone deserves a second chance. Especially when they're going through a rough patch."

Ivy seemed to consider Zoey's words, but being

humiliated in front of Emily was clearly just too much for her.

"It would have been better not to have any bracelet at all than to have had a fake one," she grumbled.

"I'm sorry that's how you feel," Zoey said. "I was only trying to help. I didn't mean to cause you problems. Really, I didn't."

"Well, you did," Ivy said, marching toward the exit. "And I can do without your 'help,' okay?"

"Okay," Zoey said to Ivy's retreating back as the bathroom door swung closed behind her.

As she walked to her next class, Zoey worried about how this was going to affect her fragile truce with Ivy. It wasn't like Ivy had gone out of her way to be nice to her, but she hadn't been mean lately, either, and it had made Zoey's life a lot more pleasant.

"Hey, Zoey?" It was Josie, the student who'd moved to Mapleton from France and was now Gabe Monaco's, Zoey's friend, girlfriend. She stopped Zoey in the hallway.

"Oh, hi, Josie," Zoey said.

"You look . . . How do you say it in English?

Like your head is in space?" Josie asked.

"Yeah, I was just thinking about something." Zoey sighed.

"I hear this thinking can be very dangerous, no?" Josie said, smiling.

Zoey laughed. "Hopefully, safer than the alternative!" she said.

"I have a favor to ask you—I saw the *très* hip bracelets you made for Libby, Priti, and Kate, and I was hoping you could make one for me too," Josie said. "I'd like to have my own special design, like you did for them."

"I can do that," Zoey said.

"I know a bunch of other girls who want them too," Josie said. "You could start a Sew Zoey accessory line."

"Um . . . yeah. I don't know, maybe," Zoey said. "But . . . right now I have to get to class."

As she rushed down the hallway to beat the bell, Zoey thought about how the bracelet Zoey gave Ivy caused nothing but trouble, but Josie was begging Zoey to make some for her and her friends. The key, Zoey thought, was that Josie wanted her bracelet to be different from the branded ones, to be special and personal. With such demand, and the cost of the booth expenses hanging over her head, selling unique versions of the bracelets began to sound like a very good option, even if they *were* copies.

CHAPTER 7

Minds and Manners

Have you done something because you were trying to be nice, but it ended up going wrong, and then the person you were trying to be nice to thought you were doing it for completely different reasons? Like, not-nice reasons? It feels so unfair, but it's hard to know what to do. If someone is going to think the worst about you, it seems like there's not a lot you can do to change their mind. I'm not even sure if writing an apology note would help. Hopefully, it's true that "It's the thought that counts." Isn't it?

I'm busy working on Aunt Lulu's maternity dress, plus making bracelets and sewing more sizes of the different clothing designs for the gift fair. I hope I at least make back the cost of the booth—or even better, make a profit! I gather from your answers to my question in a previous blog post that gift fairs can be a mixed bag: Sometimes they're awesome and you do really well, and other times . . . not so much. Please send awesome wishes my way!

"I've got good news!" Zoey told Ezra when they met up after school on Wednesday at Poppa's Pastry Shop. Marcus had picked Zoey up from school and given her a ride there, teasing her about her "date" the whole way.

"What's that?" Ezra asked, spooning whipped cream off his hot chocolate and into his mouth.

"I got a booth at the gift fair after all," Zoey told him. "They had a cancellation. There's just one catch: They want me to have some nonclothing items for sale, like accessories, to make my booth more gift fair–friendly."

"That's great!" Ezra exclaimed. "Do you know what you're going to sell?"

"I'm probably going to make more fabric bracelets—you've probably seen girls wearing them at school; they're really in style," Zoey said. "I've made some copies for my friends with prints that match their interests."

"That sounds cool."

"I thought so," Zoey said. "And they're easy and quick to make. But now I'm not sure if I should be making money by copying someone else's idea."

"I think it would be okay as long as they're different enough designs from the originals," Ezra said. "I mean, if someone copied my stuff, I think I'd take it as a compliment."

"Yeah, that's exactly how Daphne Shaw told me to look at it when someone copied my sari design," Zoey told him.

"Listen, if you're really worried about having enough accessories . . . What if you displayed some of my paintings at your booth? It would be a win-win, because it would make your booth more gifty looking, and I'd get a chance to sell my artwork."

Zoey was taken aback by the suggestion. She tried to hide her feelings, because she didn't want to upset Ezra, but even though she thought his paintings were cool, she didn't think they really meshed with the Sew Zoey style. She wanted the booth to reflect her style, not be a mishmash of Sew Zoey and Ezra styles. She was also worried about having to call back the gift fair organizers to ask them if it was okay to sell paintings that weren't her own, since they were so particular about what was being sold. But then she thought of something that made it seem worth it.

"I guess it would be fun to hang out together," she said finally. "But I'll have to think about it."

"Hang out?" Ezra asked.

"You know, manning the booth?" Zoey replied.

Ezra paused. "Oh. I guess I kind of figured I'd just hang the pictures and you'd do your thing. But yeah, if you want me to, I'll help you. It would be fun to hang out."

"Okay," Zoey said, trying to figure out if he was just saying it to be nice. "You know, I'm just not sure I want to rock the boat with the organizers, anyway. I'd have to ask permission to sell the paintings, and they barely admitted me as it is."

"I'll send you some photos of the paintings I'd want to display, just in case you decide to call them," Ezra said.

"Okay," Zoey agreed.

Now what? she thought. Doing the gift fair was becoming more complicated by the minute!

At lunch the next day, she asked her friends what they would do.

"It's not that I don't like his paintings," she explained, having received Ezra's photos by e-mail before school. "I really do. It's just . . . they're not exactly . . . Sew Zoey-ish, if you know what I mean. And if I'm going to take a risk by spending all this money to rent a booth, I want it to look like the Sew Zoey blog came to life."

"Hold on!" Priti exclaimed. "Why wouldn't you let your crush display his paintings? It'll give you the perfect excuse to hang out!"

"That's what I thought at first," Zoey said. "It turns out *he* thought he was just going to leave them there and let me do all the work—until I mentioned hanging out, and then he said he would, and yeah, it would be fun. But I don't want him to feel like he's forced into it."

"I think you should stick to your original vision," Kate said. "If he's really into you, he'll come visit, anyway."

"Okay, so one for and one against," Zoey said. "What do you think, Libby?"

Libby, who'd been crunching on carrot sticks during the discussion, swallowed and shrugged.

"I don't know," she said. "Maybe it would be cool to let Ezra show his paintings and spend time together. But I can see how you're laying out all the money for the booth and want it to look perfect. So, basically, I'm no help."

"When do you have to decide?" Kate asked.

"Soon!" Zoey said. "Like, today, since I need

to get permission, and the gift fair is a week from Friday! Plus, I still haven't decided exactly what to do for accessories. I've made some that I'll sell, but I don't like them as much as the bracelets, and I don't think there's enough variety."

"You will figure it all out," Libby said. "You always do."

It was true. Zoey did find ways to make things work. But there was always a first time for disaster, and Zoey was worried.

"Why are you so grumpy faced?" Marcus asked when Zoey walked in after school. "Cheer up, little sister!"

"I can't," Zoey complained. "I'm stressing out about the gift fair. I don't know what to do."

"What's the problem?" Marcus asked. "I thought you got a booth? And you just have to make some accessories, right? Piece of cake."

"I know." Zoey sighed. "But the only accessories I've made lately that I really like are those fabric bracelets."

"What's wrong with those?" Marcus asked.

"Didn't you say your friends loved them and wear them every day?"

"Yeah," Zoey replied. "But they're copies, basically. I'm going in circles trying to decide if I'm okay with selling them. Anyway, the real problem is that when I told Ezra all this, he suggested I sell his paintings in the booth as gifts, instead. And I'm not sure if I want to. But I don't want to hurt his feelings, either."

"*Awkward.* Trouble in paradise already," Marcus joked. Then, seeing that Zoey really wasn't in the mood for humor, he asked, "So what are the pros and cons?"

Zoey filled him in on the good and bad points of letting Ezra display his work.

Marcus drummed on the table with his fingers. It was a family joke that he always seemed to think better when he was drumming.

"Zo, I think you should stay true to yourself and say no. Maybe offer to call and see if he can get his own booth or something," Marcus suggested. "If he likes you enough, he'll understand."

"That's a great idea!" Zoey said, feeling like a

weight had lifted from her. "Thanks, Marcus!"

"Well, now that I've solved that problem . . . How are things going with you and Allie?" Marcus asked. "Last time she was here, things seemed tense."

"Oh, that," Zoey said. She hadn't wanted to mention Allie to her brother, but she was still worried. "Well, we're both selling accessories, so we made a No Weirdness Pact."

"Uh . . . what's that?"

"Basically, we agreed to have fun and not make the gift fair sales a competition," Zoey explained.

"That sounds like a good plan," Marcus said.

"If we can keep to it," Zoey said. "The thing is, Allie and I were never supercompetitive before, but things feel different ever since you guys broke up, even though we're trying to get things back to normal."

"I'm sorry that what happened with Allie and me seems to have messed up your friendship," Marcus said.

"I don't know if our friendship will ever be the same, but I'm willing to try—and so is Allie."

"Well, I hope it works," Marcus said. "I really do."

"You know what? Talking to you has helped me make up my mind," Zoey told her brother. "I'm going to go ahead and make more bracelets to sell. And I'm going to tell Ezra no."

She wasn't looking forward to that last thing at all. Not at all.

CHAPTER 8

From Copied to Copycat

I'm busy making bracelets for the gift fair, where I'm going to have a stall for the first time. If you're one of my friends, teachers, or parents reading this, please come by and check out the clothes and gifts—perfect for all your present-giving needs! These bracelets aren't exactly like the ones you can buy for a lot more in the boutiques. But people at school—well, at least most of the people at school—seem to like them, anyway.

I know there's debate in the fashion world about producing knockoffs of other designs, but like my mentor told me, "Imitation is a form of flattery." I've been "flattered," and now I'm hoping I'll be flattering other designers. As long as I'm putting my own special twist on the design, I think it's okay. . . . Do you? I sometimes wish there was a rule book with all the fashion laws written out, like the rules of the road.

"I can't wait to see the maternity dress you've made for me," Aunt Lulu said when Zoey, Marcus, and Dad arrived for dinner on Friday evening.

Her aunt's baby bump had really expanded since Zoey had last seen her, and Aunt Lulu had also developed a bit of a waddle.

"I hope it fits," Zoey said. "I mean, I made it with plenty of extra room for the baby . . . at least I think I did . . . but I'm not exactly an expert when it comes to making maternity clothes!"

"Thanks, honey," Aunt Lulu said. "I take it you noticed my new duck walk."

"My adorable duckling," Uncle John said.

Aunt Lulu swatted him, but she was smiling.

"Stop! You're driving me quackers!" she said.

"You guys are quacking me up," Marcus said.

"I love this family," Uncle John said. "I hope the baby inherits its quacky sense of humor."

Aunt Lulu groaned.

"Let's see this dress, Zo," she begged. "I want to try it on *before* I eat and feel any bigger than I do now!"

They all trooped into the living room—with Aunt Lulu waddling a few steps behind—and Zoey pulled the dress out of the fancy shopping bag she'd carried it in, neatly folded and wrapped in tissue, so it didn't wrinkle.

"I love it!" Aunt Lulu exclaimed. "It's totally adorable! Come upstairs so I can try it on. I'll give you a sneak peek of your cousin-to-be's room while we're up there."

Zoey helped zip Aunt Lulu into the dress. It fit . . . but snugly.

"I thought I'd left *so much* extra room," Zoey said in despair. "But there's none at all!"

"You didn't count on your cousin here being a super-duper fast grower!" Aunt Lulu said, rubbing her belly lovingly.

She looked at herself in the mirror and smiled at Zoey.

"Still, it fits me *now*, and that's what counts. I can't grow that much between tonight and Sunday, so it'll be fine!"

Zoey helped unzip the dress, and after her aunt had changed back into her previous outfit, Aunt Lulu took her to see the nursery. It was painted a peaceful, pale shade of butter yellow. There was a gray glider and matching ottoman, and a white crib with yellow and gray bedding. Over the crib hung letters of the alphabet painted the same yellow as the walls, and over the changing table, Zoey spotted adorable photos of her aunt and uncle when they were babies. Then she saw a white tree-shaped bookshelf stocked with *Goodnight Moon*; *Pat the Bunny*; *Good Night, Gorilla*; *Mr. Brown Can Moo! Can You?*; and other books.

"I love these books!" Zoey said.

"I know! I remember reading them to you when you were little. Call me crazy, but I've been reading to my little niblet already," Aunt Lulu said, patting her belly. "It seems to stop the nighttime gymnastics that keep me awake at two in the morning."

"Do you think Niblet understands?" Zoey asked, curious.

"I wouldn't go that far," Aunt Lulu said. "But I like to think the baby can hear my voice and is calmed by it."

She winced and rubbed her side. "Speaking of the baby, I just got a foot in the rib cage. Do you want to feel your cousin moving?"

"Sure," Zoey said, although to tell the truth, she was a little freaked out by the idea.

Aunt Lulu took Zoey's hand and placed it on her round belly.

"Hold on a sec. It won't be long. . . . There!"

Sure enough, Zoey felt a movement under her hand, where Aunt Lulu's belly suddenly got very hard and firm and then softened again.

"What was that?" Zoey asked.

"Not sure if it was an elbow or a foot," Aunt Lulu said. "All I know is that there are certain times during the day that I get a constant rat-a-tat-tat going in there. Marcus might have a little drummer on his hands. I'm not sure I can handle that! Maybe the calm of the baby's room will help keep things mellow."

"I love it," Zoey said. "It's perfect. Niblet's lucky to have an interior designer for a mom."

"And to have a cousin like you," Aunt Lulu said, putting her arm around Zoey and hugging her. "You know, Zo, even though I'm having this baby, I'll always think of you as my first daughter—since your mom died—and I will always be there for you. The baby won't change that."

Before she even knew what hit her, Zoey's eyes welled with tears, and a lump formed in her throat. She turned and threw her arms around Aunt Lulu and hugged her. Well, as much as she could around the bump of her cousin-to-be, which was an ever-present reminder between them.

"Hey, I didn't mean to upset you," Aunt Lulu said, stroking her hair.

"You d-didn't." Zoey sniffed. "You made me h-happy."

Aunt Lulu smiled. "John's right. We are a strange family. We cry when we're happy!"

Zoey laughed through her tears. "I guess I didn't know I was worried about it until you said that," she explained. "But now I feel so much better."

"Good," Aunt Lulu said. "Now let's go have some dinner. I'm eating for two, and I'm ravenous!"

Zoey and Ezra met at the library on Saturday morning to see one of the free movies they were showing in the auditorium.

"Hey, did you get a chance to ask the gift fair organizers about including my paintings?" Ezra asked before the movie started.

"Yeah . . . about that," Zoey said. "I thought about it, and I just felt like it would be unprofessional of me to ask them when I didn't include your paintings in my original submission. The other thing is . . . Well, even though I really love your art, it doesn't really match my Sew Zoey clothes and accessories, if you know what I mean."

She glanced at Ezra anxiously to see his reaction. "Are you upset?"

"No, I understand," he said. "Maybe a little disappointed. I was looking forward to hanging out."

"Well, we can still hang out. And how about I call the organizers and see if there are any small booths left so that you could have one of your own?" Zoey offered. "That way you could display your stuff, and we'd still get to hang out a little bit."

"You'd be okay with doing that?"

"Sure. I'll do it when I get home."

Ezra smiled. "Thanks, Zoey. You're the best!"

Zoey smiled back as the lights dimmed. Now that she knew Ezra wasn't upset with her, she could actually relax and enjoy the movie!

When she got home later that afternoon, she called Mrs. Perry, the gift fair organizer, to ask about the availability of a small booth for Ezra.

"I'm afraid there aren't any booths left," Mrs. Perry said. "You got the very last one."

"Oh," Zoey said, crestfallen. "That's too bad. My friend was really looking forward to it."

"Definitely have him apply next year," Mrs. Perry suggested. "And tell him to think about having some of his work printed on greeting cards. Those always sell well at the fair."

"That's a good idea," Zoey said. "Thanks, I'll tell him."

As soon as she hung up, she called Ezra to tell him the news.

"It's too bad about the booth," she said. "But you should definitely try next year. And what do you think about doing the greeting cards?"

"I'll think about it," Ezra said. "It sounds great."

"That's what I thought," Zoey said. "I bet you'd sell lots of them!"

"Hey, are you going to be home in an hour?" Ezra asked.

"Yeah," Zoey said. "I have to make more bracelets for the gift fair."

"Is it okay if I stop by to drop something off?"

"What is it?" Zoey asked.

"If I tell you, it won't be a surprise," Ezra said.

"Sure, it's okay," Zoey said. "But now I'm dying of curiosity!"

"I'll be there soon!"

The hour passed really slowly as Zoey tried to concentrate on making bracelets and not wonder what Ezra was bringing over. Finally, the doorbell rang, and she ran to answer it.

Ezra stood there holding a small painting.

"I brought this for you," he said. "Thanks for trying to get me a booth."

"That's so sweet!" Zoey said. "I'm really sorry it didn't work out."

"Well, I appreciate you making the call," Ezra said. "I'll apply next year. Anyway, I better run. I just wanted to give this to you."

"Thanks, I love it!" Zoey called to him as he ran back to the car where his dad waited.

The painting was a small autumn landscape, and the colors were bright yellows and reds and golds against the earthy browns of tree trunks. Looking at it, Zoey suddenly had a wonderful idea: She could take the digital photographs of Ezra's paintings and screen print them onto scarves and headbands to sell at her booth as a surprise for Ezra. That way, she'd have more accessories and he'd get more exposure for his art. She could even give him the profits from the sales, because they'd be printed with his artwork.

It seemed like the perfect solution to both problems. She couldn't wait to see his reaction. She loved his surprise. She hoped he would love hers.

"This is the first baby shower I've ever been to," Marcus said as they walked up to the door to Aunt Lulu and Uncle John's house, which was decorated with yellow, white, and silver balloons. "Well, except for mine, and I don't remember much about that."

"I haven't been to many myself," Dad said. "They used to be ladies-only affairs, but I guess the times they are a-changing."

"Why shouldn't it be coed?" Zoey asked. "If both parents are supposed to look after the baby, then they both should have a party."

"True," Dad said.

When Aunt Lulu answered the door, Zoey noticed right away that she wasn't wearing the outfit she'd made.

"Come on in!" Lulu said.

Zoey handed her the gift bag containing the sweet baby outfit she'd made for her new cousin, and Dad handed Lulu the very professionally wrapped present he'd told them the Mystery Lady had chosen—even though she'd decided not to come to the shower.

Aunt Lulu kissed them all.

"Where's Buttons?" Zoey asked as she looked around for her aunt's adorable dog, who usually greeted Zoey at the door.

"He's at doggie day care today, since there are so many people here for the party. Let's go join them," she said. "Your new cousin-to-be is the star attraction. I've never had so many people touching my stomach in my life!"

Zoey watched her aunt entertaining her friends, laughing as they felt the baby move under their hands. She desperately wanted to ask Aunt Lulu why she wasn't wearing the dress, but with her aunt and the bump being the center of attention—not to mention the hostess with the mostest—it was impossible to get a quiet moment to pose the question.

Already a little worried about being relegated to second place when the baby arrived, Zoey wondered if Aunt Lulu would be able to keep her promise that she'd still consider Zoey as her first daughter. She tried to push the thought out of her mind and enjoy the party—after all, this was *Aunt Lulu*, who had always been wonderful and loving toward her. But why wasn't Aunt Lulu wearing the dress? Was she lying when she said she liked it? It wasn't like her aunt to lie to her, but everything seemed to be changing at the moment.

"You look way too serious for a baby shower," Uncle John said. "Have a cupcake!"

"They look great," Zoey said, taking a yellow frosted cupcake.

"They taste pretty good, too," Uncle John said, winking. "I had to eat one for quality control."

Zoey giggled and took a bite. It was good.

"Don't go anywhere with those cupcakes before I get one," Marcus warned, walking over from the other side of the room, followed closely by Dad.

"Me too," Dad said. "I've been eyeing those since we got here."

Uncle John offered them each a cupcake, then said, "I better go circulate before the Webber family decimates dessert."

As he walked off, Marcus said, "I can't believe your girlfriend wouldn't come to this, Dad. Wouldn't she want to join you since it's such a special family occasion?"

Zoey watched her dad's face take on the familiar pained expression he got whenever they talked about meeting the Mystery Lady.

"She wanted to come," Dad said. "She was really conflicted about it, because this could be her future niece. I mean—"

He stopped, seeing Marcus and Zoey exchange shocked glances.

"You can't be seriously considering marrying someone you haven't even introduced us to yet, can you?" Marcus asked.

"Yeah, if you get married to someone we've never met, Marcus and I might just have to think about boycotting the wedding!" Zoey protested, only half joking.

"Listen, I would never think about marrying

someone without you guys meeting her and liking her," Dad said.

"But . . . you said 'future niece,'" Marcus pointed out.

"We do like each other . . . a lot," Dad admitted. "I won't lie to you. It is potentially serious, but there are no solid plans, okay? And these kinds of conversations happen in relationships. But you guys are my number-one priority, always. That's why it's so important to me that you both like her."

"It's kind of hard to like someone you've never met," Zoey said.

Dad laughed.

"You will meet her. Soon," he said. "And *definitely* before there are any real talks of marriage!"

"Okay, everyone!" Aunt Lulu announced. "It's time to open the presents!"

Everyone gathered around in the living room, and Marcus and Zoey took turns handing Aunt Lulu presents while Uncle John kept a careful list of who gave what, so they could write thank-you notes.

"Zoey, this is just too cute for words!" Aunt Lulu exclaimed when she held up the outfit and hooded bath towel Zoey made. "Everyone, my incredibly talented niece made these! She's been on TV, you know!"

Zoey blushed but was secretly pleased by how proud Aunt Lulu was of her.

Marcus handed Aunt Lulu the very beautifully wrapped present from Dad.

"This is from Dad," he said. "But you know he didn't wrap it. The Mystery Lady did."

"She chose it, too," Dad admitted.

Aunt Lulu opened the box and took out an adorable onesie with a bunny motif and a matching hat, and a hand-knit baby blanket. Zoey was impressed.

"Well, I have to give the Mystery Lady points for good taste," she said.

"Oh, she has really good taste," Aunt Lulu agreed.

"Wait, you've met her?" Marcus asked.

"We have," Uncle John said.

"She's great," Aunt Lulu assured them. "You guys are going to love her. I promise you."

"Yeah, if we ever get to meet her," Marcus grumbled.

"Patience, grasshopper. You will," Aunt Lulu said.

"I know. Sorry, Aunt Lulu," Marcus said.

"It's okay, honey, I understand," Aunt Lulu said. "Now hand me the next present."

When all the presents were unwrapped, and everyone had placed their bets on the birth date and sex of the baby, it was time to go. As Zoey was about to leave, Aunt Lulu waddled over to say good-bye and took her aside.

"Zoey, honey, I wanted to apologize for not wearing the dress you made for me to the shower. You see . . . Niblet here must have had a little growth spurt between Friday and this morning, because I put on the dress and then, when I sat down before the party to put my feet up and rest my swollen ankles, I heard this great big riiiiippppp!" she explained. "And what do you know! My entire backside was hanging out when I got up!"

"Oh no!" Zoey exclaimed.

"Oh yes!" Aunt Lulu said. "Thank goodness it happened *before* the guests arrived!"

"And that you had a backup dress," Zoey said.

"That too. The doctors are actually thinking of moving my due date up because the baby is growing so fast," Aunt Lulu said. "Anyway, I wanted to tell you earlier, but I got all tied up with party things."

"I'm just glad that it wasn't because you didn't like the dress," Zoey said.

"Of course not! I love the dress! In fact, I was hoping you can fix it to make it into a loose comfy dress for after the baby is born," Aunt Lulu said.

"Sure, I can do that," Zoey said. "Where is it? I'll take it home now and see what I can do."

"It's upstairs on the bed in our room. Thanks, Zo," Aunt Lulu said. "I look forward to the day I can wear it!"

CHAPTER 9

*Bear*y Cute!

Aunt Lulu's shower was a blast—so many adorable little baby clothes and tiny little cupcakes. Still no clues about if I'm having a boy or a girl cousin—Aunt Lulu purposely picked a "gender neutral" color scheme of white and yellow for everything, from the table decorations, to the flowers to the cupcake frosting! Aunt Lulu and Uncle John loved the beary cute things I made for the baby, I'm happy to report. And I have learned something about Dad's Mystery Lady, though— she has good fashion sense, at least in baby clothes. ☺ The outfit she picked out for my cousin-to-be was really cute.

Now that the shower is over, I'm full speed ahead getting everything made and ready for the gift fair next weekend. It's going to be all sewing and accessory making, all the time. Wish me luck!

When Zoey checked her e-mail after school on Monday she was thrilled to see Daphne Shaw's name in her in-box—and even more excited when she read the e-mail:

> Zoey,
>
> I LOVED the second batch of items you sent— so much so that I couldn't just pick one thing to feature in the pop-up store: I'm going to have to feature two items instead. I really like the flared

skirt and the origami-inspired top. What do you think? Can you manage to produce two pieces for me? I'd need five pieces in each size to start.

Best,

Daphne

Zoey e-mailed back right away.

Hi, Daphne!

When does the store open? As soon as you let me know, I'll let you know if I can do it! But I'd do just about anything to make this happen! ☺

Zoey

She was itching to start sewing, but figured she should wait to hear from Daphne. Luckily, the designer responded within minutes.

Silly me! The pop-up shop launch is in three weeks' time—on Saturday evening. And I'd love for you to come to the grand opening! I think you're ready for the red carpet.

Red carpet? That sounded amazing!

Zoey wrote back:

> I think I can get the pieces ready in time. I have to see if someone can bring me to the opening. But I definitely *want* to come!

When Dad got home, she told him the good news.

"So, can you take me to the opening?" she asked. "I'd normally ask Aunt Lulu, because I know these fashion events are more her thing, but with the baby-to-be and everything . . ."

"Good thinking," Dad said. "Let me check the football schedule."

Zoey's dad was a physical therapist for the local university team and had to be available to treat the players before and after games. He looked at his calendar and frowned.

"I'm sorry, honey, we've got an away game on Saturday afternoon. I wouldn't be able to get back in time to get you up to New York."

Seeing Zoey's crestfallen face, he continued,

"Why don't you ask Lulu? I know she's getting close, but knowing your aunt, I bet she'd enjoy a night on the red carpet before the baby comes."

"I hadn't thought of that," Zoey said. "I'll give her a call."

Aunt Lulu was thrilled to hear Zoey's exciting news.

"I'm so proud of you, honey. And I wish like anything that I could take you to strut down the catwalk at the opening. Or in my case, waddle down the catwalk," Aunt Lulu said. "But I saw the doctor this morning, and he told me to take it easy and stick close to home. I guess just to be safe, since I'm getting close-ish to the due date."

"Oh . . . ," Zoey said, trying to hide the disappointment from her voice. "I understand."

"I hope you find someone who can take you," Aunt Lulu said. "I'd hate if you had to miss the chance to be there on your big day!"

Zoey sighed. "Me too!" she said.

As disappointed as Zoey was, she didn't have any time to sit around and feel sorry for herself. With the gift fair opening in a few days, there was just too much to do. She spent Tuesday and Wednesday after school making more bracelets out of a variety of fabrics, and making scarves and headbands with fabric she'd screen printed with images of Ezra's painting. She was so happy with the way they were looking that she wanted him to see. She asked Ezra if he wanted to video chat, saying that she had a surprise for him.

"So what's the big surprise?" he asked when they were both on camera.

"Well, I felt bad about the fact that you couldn't get a booth at the gift fair, and I loved the painting you gave me as a gift so much that it gave me an idea," Zoey explained. "I figured out a way that I could have more accessories to sell, and you could get more exposure for your art."

She held up one of the silk-screened scarves. "What do you think?"

"Wait—that's my painting," Ezra said.

"I know!" Zoey said. "That's the surprise!"

"Oh." Ezra's face looked blank.

To Zoey's dismay, while Ezra did seem genuinely

surprised, he *didn't* seem all that happy.

"What's the matter?" she asked. "I thought you'd like it."

Ezra hesitated. "I . . . well . . . I think of my paintings as art. Not as decoration for other things."

"It *is* art," Zoey said. "But you can buy clothes and T-shirts and scarves with famous paintings on them at art museum gift stores, right?"

"Yes, but . . . I guess I'm also kind of upset that you didn't ask me first."

"The only reason I didn't ask you was because I wanted to do this as a surprise," Zoey said. "And because you seemed to think copying is a compliment. But I guess I should have asked you, now that I think about it. And the other thing is that I plan to give you all the profits from the headbands and scarves."

"I don't know," Ezra said.

"Also, I can get my brother, Marcus, to make a stack of postcards to hand out at the booth—he's really good at graphic design," Zoey said, hoping to make Ezra feel better about everything. "That way people who like the painting on the accessories will know where to find you to buy original artwork."

"Look, Zoey, I get that you were trying to do something nice for me, because of the booth thing, and that's really sweet," Ezra said. "But I'm still not sure how I feel about my paintings being used on accessories. I have to think about it."

"Okay, I understand," Zoey said, although she wasn't sure she did. "Just . . . Can you let me know soon? Because if I can't use these, I have to make something else and the fair starts on Friday."

"Yeah. I'll let you know tomorrow," Ezra said.

When Zoey hung up, she panicked. Why if Ezra said no to the scarves and headbands? She'd already made a bunch, and then she'd still need something else besides bracelets to sell as accessories. And time was running out!

By lunch the next day, Zoey still hadn't heard anything from Ezra, and she was starting to freak out.

"Why hasn't he let me know yet?" she wailed. "The gift fair setup is tomorrow! Even if I can think of something else to sell, I'm not going to have enough time to make enough of whatever it is!"

"I know you wanted this to be a surprise," Kate said. "But you really should have asked Ezra first."

"Yeah, I can kind of understand why he's miffed," Libby said. "How would you feel if Allie had taken one of your designs and put it on a tote bag without asking you?"

"I would be upset," Zoey admitted. "Listen, I know *now* that I should have asked Ezra first."

"But it's too late now," Priti said. "He's already upset."

"And I have to set up my booth tomorrow after school," Zoey said. "What am I going to do if he says no?"

Her friends all looked at her sadly.

"I wish I had a great idea to help, but I don't," Kate said.

"Me neither," Libby agreed. "Not on such short notice."

"I just hope he says yes," Priti said.

"You and me both," Zoey said, hoping like anything that he'd let her know—soon! She decided to make some infinity scarves and headbands out of fabric from her stash after school, just in case.

Zoey had just finished sewing her third infinity scarf out of conflict-free fabric when Ezra finally called.

"Oh, hey, Ezra," Zoey said. "I've been on pins and needles waiting to hear from you. So . . . have you made a decision yet? What do you think? Are you okay with me selling the scarves and headbands?"

"Well, I guess it's okay this time," Ezra said, and Zoey felt a huge weight of worry disappear. "But I still wish you'd asked me first."

"I know! So do I!" Zoey said. "I realize now that it was kind of silly of me not to."

"For one thing, I probably would have chosen different paintings if I'd known they were going to be on accessories," Ezra said. "It would have been good to have some input."

"I understand," Zoey said. "And I'm really sorry."

"So I was thinking—it's not really fair for me to take all the profits from the silk-screen accessories," Ezra said. "I mean, yeah it's my painting, but making the accessories was your idea. Plus, you had to spend all the time designing and silk-screening and sewing. So, I say we split the profits."

"Are you sure?" Zoey asked.

"I'm one hundred percent sure that I should only get fifty percent of the profits," Ezra said.

"I'll agree to that if you agree to come keep me company at the gift fair," Zoey said.

"Fine—as long as I don't have to wear a scarf or a headband!" Ezra said.

"Well, then," Zoey said. "You've got yourself a deal!"

She breathed a sigh of relief when they hung up, and made a few headbands out of the stash fabric, too, so the display would look balanced. She was finally getting excited!

Friday after school, Zoey packed up all of her merchandise, and Dad and Marcus drove her to the gift fair location to set up her booth. Allie was already there, having driven straight from school, and her booth was mostly set up.

"Wow, it looks great, Allie!" Zoey said as she passed, carrying a box of accessories.

"Thanks," Allie said. "Good luck setting up yours."

"Where do I get all my display materials?" Zoey asked.

"Whatever you ordered should be in the booth," Allie said.

Then Allie spotted Marcus, who was helping Mr. Webber bring in more of Zoey's boxes of merchandise on a hand truck. Zoey saw Allie quickly turn away to rearrange some handbags that were on hooks attached to the side of the tent.

Awkward, Zoey thought. *Will it ever get less weird between Allie and Marcus? Maybe they need a No Weirdness Pact of their own!* But she didn't have time to worry. There was too much to get done setting up her booth.

But when Zoey looked in her booth, there wasn't much there in the way of hooks and display shelves. Everything she ordered definitely wasn't there.

"What am I going to do?" Zoey asked Dad and Marcus, her voice rising in panic.

"The first thing you're going to do is not freak out," Dad said. "And then we'll go over and ask the organizers what happened to the rest of your order."

At the organizers' table, Dad nudged Zoey to do the talking.

"I don't seem to have all of my display order," Zoey said. "And it's a real problem, especially because I didn't get a clothing rack, so I'm not sure how I'm going to display my garments properly."

"I know. We had a problem with the delivery," Mrs. Perry said. "The display company didn't deliver our order in full, so we've had to cut back on what we're giving people based on what they ordered. I'm really sorry for the inconvenience."

Zoey realized that she should have ordered more display items like Allie told her. Trying to save money on display materials now meant she was going to be extra short.

"What am I supposed to do?" Zoey asked.

"You might try asking around to see if any of the other vendors have stuff they're not using," said Mrs. Perry. "Sometimes they order more than they need, just in case."

"I'll go back and help Marcus unpack the boxes while you go talk to the vendors," Dad said.

Zoey felt embarrassed having to ask people she

didn't know if they had spare display materials. She decided to ask Allie first, because she was her friend. But when she explained the situation, Allie said, "That's why I said to order extra."

"I will next time!" Zoey promised. "But can you help me out now?"

Allie looked around her booth.

"I *suppose* I can combine these key chains and change purses on to the large display shelf," Allie said. "Then you can have the small shelf. And I have one small hanging rod to spare. But I can't really spare anything else."

Zoey felt mad, even though she knew it wasn't Allie's fault that she was short on materials. If anything, it was her own. But Allie didn't have to be mean about it. That wasn't like her; at least not like the girl Zoey had become friends with.

"Well, thanks for that," Zoey said. "I'm going to ask other vendors to see if I can scrounge up anything else."

After a begging tour of the booths, Zoey had managed to come away with an odd assortment of display things but was still way short of what she needed. She came back to the booth, and with Marcus and Dad's help, tried to arrange what she had so it looked good.

"The booth still looks half empty, and I don't have anything else to display my stuff with," Zoey complained. "What am I going to do?"

"How about if Dad and I go to the hardware store and see what we can pick up there?" Marcus suggested.

"Isn't that going to be expensive?" Zoey asked. She was beginning to wish she'd never signed up for the gift fair.

"Don't worry," Dad said. "I'll cover it. Or maybe we can ask the organizers to reimburse us, since they didn't get everything you needed and they still charged you. But really, honey, I'm happy to buy it."

Zoey stayed and laid out the bracelets neatly in the wooden trays she'd made in industrial arts and tried to decorate the booth as best she could.

While Dad and Marcus were gone, Mrs. Perry came around to see how Zoey was doing.

"Not so good," Zoey said. "But my dad and

brother have gone to the hardware store to find some racks and shelves."

"Oh dear. . . . These booths are made such that the shelves and display racks fit in a very specific way," Mrs. Perry warned. "I'm not sure if other racks and shelves will work with it."

"Should I call Dad and tell him to forget about it?" Zoey asked, worried.

"I don't know," Mrs. Perry said. "They might work. Give them a try. In the meantime, I'll see if I can call around to get you some more things locally—and also see if I can convince the other vendors to share a bit more."

"Thank you," Zoey said.

"It's the least I can do," Mrs. Perry said.

Dad and Marcus returned forty-five minutes later with hooks, racks, clothing rods, and shelves.

"This should do the trick," Dad said. "We'll have the rest of this set up in no time."

At least that's what they thought . . . until they tried to hang the first shelf.

"These hooks won't fit," Marcus said.

Dad examined the small shelf that Allie had let Zoey borrow.

"It looks like there's a special fitting on the end of this that matches the wall of the booth," he said. "I didn't see anything like this at the hardware store."

"Thanks for trying, guys. But Mrs. Perry said it might not work," Zoey wailed. "And she was right. Now what do we do?"

"I guess maybe we could try affixing the clothes with duct tape," Dad suggested. "Maybe it would look cool in a gritty way?"

"What?" Zoey exclaimed. "No way! That would look awful!" She didn't mean to snap at her dad, but the idea of taping clothes up with duct tape made her cringe.

"Yeah, I'm seconding Zoey on vetoing that duct tape idea," Marcus agreed. "It would look really unprofessional."

"Well, any other ideas?" Dad asked. "'Cause I've got nothing."

"I know! Let's call Aunt Lulu," Marcus suggested. "She's done lots of trade shows. I bet she'll know how to improvise."

"Good thinking!" Zoey said. She pushed the speed dial for her aunt.

"Hey, Zo!" Aunt Lulu said. "How's the booth looking?"

"It's a bit of a disaster at the moment," Zoey said. She explained about the delivery shortage and the problem with hanging the shelves and the clothing rods on to the booth wall.

"They're supposed to have a special bracket in order to fit on to the booth," Zoey explained. "And the ones from the hardware store don't."

"I bet zip ties would work for the smaller shelves if they have predrilled holes in them for brackets or nails," Aunt Lulu suggested. "And they're a lot more discreet than duct tape. Tell your dad I'm with you on that!"

"I know, right?" Zoey said. "Black zip ties are a great idea."

"But those probably aren't strong enough to hold the clothing rods," Aunt Lulu said. "Especially once you have them loaded up with clothes. I'm not sure what to do about those."

"Well, thanks for the zip ties idea," Zoey said.

"Hopefully, we'll figure out to do with the rods."

"Oh! Or you also could use twine to make a clothesline cross the booth, and hang things from it with wooden clothespins," Aunt Lulu suggested. "It's a simple solution that looks cute and rustic."

When Zoey hung up, she explained to Dad and Marcus what Aunt Lulu said about the zip ties, clothespins, and the clothing rods.

"I can run back to the hardware store and pick up some zip ties," Dad said. "And the wooden clothespins and twine. But the clothing rods are still a problem. Do you really need them?"

"Yes!" Zoey said. "The twine is a great idea, but clothes are heavy, so I can't hang too many pieces on each line. And if I have too many clotheslines in the booth, it's going to look messy instead of cute."

"Wait! I think I've just had a brainstorm for what to do with those," Marcus said. "Do we have any ladders at home?"

"Yeah," Dad said. "I've got one or two old ones hanging around in the garage. They aren't in great shape, though."

"That's okay," Marcus said. "Just bring them when you come back with the zip ties."

"What do you want ladders for?" Zoey asked.

"Wait and see," Marcus said, which was annoyingly mysterious, but Zoey didn't mind as long as his idea worked!

When Dad came back from his errand, he asked Marcus for help. They returned carrying two old wooden ladders.

"I've been meaning to get rid of these ever since I bought the aluminum ladder, but luckily for you, they were still in the garage," Dad said.

"They're perfect!" Marcus exclaimed.

"Perfect for what?" Zoey asked.

"Watch and learn," Marcus said. He propped open the two ladders, then took one of the clothing rods and rested it across the ladders' steps. "Ta-da!" he said, picking up another one and resting it on a lower step. "Your clothing rack!"

"Wow! That's such a great idea!" Zoey exclaimed. "It looks . . . rustic, which will tie in perfectly with the twine clothesline and wooden pegs!"

She started hanging clothes on the rods while

Dad and Marcus strung up the twine and tied the clothing rods to the ladders to keep them stable.

"Good thinking on the ladders," Dad told Marcus.

"Just being a good brother," Marcus said, grinning.

When Zoey finished arranging all her stuff, it turned out she didn't even need the things she'd borrowed from Allie and the other vendors, so she went around and returned them. Between Marcus and Aunt Lulu, they'd solved her problem *and* created a cool, rustic look for her booth.

"Our make-do booth looks better than how I designed it!" Zoey said.

"Teamwork," Dad said, putting his arms around Zoey and Marcus. "The Webber family makes a great team!"

---------- CHAPTER 10 ----------

Fashion Hardware

Aunt Lulu often uses the phrase "necessity is the mother of invention," but it was never more true than this afternoon, when we were setting up my booth for the gift fair! I thought we wouldn't have enough display items to show off the things I've worked so hard to make in a way that looks attractive and will make people want to buy them. But between Aunt Lulu, Dad, and especially Marcus, my day was saved! We rigged up twine and clothespins to hang up lines to display some items, and then Marcus had the brainstorm to use two old ladders as a base for the clothing rods, creating the perfect rustic-looking rack. All's well that ends well! And I got an idea for hardware-store inspired clothing made of nuts and bolts (fabric bolts, that is). It was a win-win!

Dad dropped Zoey off early the next day, so she could be in her booth before the gift fair opened. Zoey looked for Allie on the way over, but she didn't seem to be in hers yet.

The first hour was very slow. There weren't many people at the fair, and the ones who were there didn't seem interested in what she had to offer. It was really depressing to watch people walk straight by her booth with barely a glance.

Zoey started to worry that the whole days was going to be a total failure and she'd end up losing money on the booth rental. That would mean less money to buy fabrics for all her other ideas.

Just as she was starting to despair, a girl walked by the booth, saw the fabric bracelets, and stopped.

"Wow!" she said. "You have so many more designs than they sell in the store!"

"That's because I make them myself," Zoey explained. "They're not the name brand."

"I don't care if they're the name brand," the girl said. "I totally love your designs."

I wish Ivy felt that way, Zoey thought.

"I'm going to get this one," the girl said, picking out a bracelet with a sunflower design.

"Thanks for being my first sale!" Zoey said, taking her money. "Do you want a bag?"

"No, I'm just going to wear it right now. It's a gift from me to me!" the girl said.

Zoey laughed. "Well, enjoy wearing it!"

Shortly afterward, an older woman came up and started browsing.

"These are just beautiful—and so unusual," she said, picking up one of the silk-screened scarves with Ezra's painting on it.

"My friend did the artwork," Zoey said. "Here's a card with his information if you're interested in buying one of his paintings."

She handed the woman one of the cards Marcus had designed with Ezra's details.

"Thank you," the woman said. "In the meantime, I'd like to buy this scarf for my daughter-in-law. It's just her kind of thing."

Things are starting to look up, Zoey thought. She just hoped it kept looking up enough so she'd make a profit.

She wondered if Ezra was going to stop by to hang out, and if so, when. That would definitely brighten up her day.

Just then Zoey saw a familiar face step into the booth—Jan.

"Your layout looks wonderful!" Jan said. "So creative with the ladders and the twine clothesline."

Zoey laughed. "We had to do that—because I didn't have enough display materials!"

She told Jan about the short delivery and setup hiccups from the day before.

"Well, you certainly made the best of it," Jan

said. "Now, I need to find a present for a friend. . . . What do you suggest?"

"I recommend the silk-screened scarves," Ezra said, surprising Zoey by sneaking into the booth while she was talking to Jan.

"Hi, Ezra! Have you come to help and hang out?" Zoey asked as Jan looked around.

He grinned. "At your service!"

"Ezra did the original artwork that I silk-screened onto the scarves," Zoey explained to Jan. "Here's his card."

"These are so beautiful," Jan said. "I'm not sure which one I like best!"

She ended up buying one for her friend and one for herself.

"See you in the store!" she said. "Good luck with the rest of the fair."

"Did you see? She took my card!" Ezra said. "Maybe she'll buy a painting!"

"Another customer who bought a scarf took the card too," Zoey told him.

"Thanks, Zoey," Ezra said. "This could turn out to be a pretty good thing for me. I'm sorry I freaked out."

"I'm sorry, too," Zoey said. "Because you were right—I should have asked you first."

"Hey, look—Libby and your other friends are here," Ezra said.

Sure enough, Kate, Priti, and Libby converged on the booth.

"How's it going?" Priti asked. "Are you a gazillionaire yet?"

"Um . . . I'm still a few gazillions short," Zoey admitted. "It was pretty slow earlier."

"It looked like a lot more people were arriving when Mom dropped us off," Libby said. "So hopefully things will get busier."

"The bracelets look really good," Priti said. "I'm sorry I overreacted about you copying them."

"It's okay," Zoey said. "I understand."

"Hey, do you mind if I go look around before it gets too busy?" Ezra asked. "I haven't seen any of the fair yet."

"Sure—I got to go around and look yesterday when I was scrounging for display materials," Zoey said.

"The booth looks amazing," Kate said. "And the

scarves and headbands with Ezra's art came out so well!"

"Let's go look at the rest of the fair with Ezra, then we'll come back," Priti suggested.

The four of them trooped off to look around, and Zoey sold a few more bracelets and a headband in the meantime. She also had another visitor: Ivy, who stood by the booth, looking awkward.

"Hey, Ivy," Zoey said. "How do you like the gift fair?"

"It's pretty good," Ivy said. She glanced over at the display of bracelets. "Listen, Zoey, I . . . want to say . . . well, I'm sorry about how I acted when I found out the bracelet wasn't the store brand. I was just really embarrassed when Emily called me out on it in industrial arts in front of everyone. Plus, I really thought it was the real deal. It looked really good."

"It's okay," Zoey said. "I was just trying to do something to make your life easier."

"I know," Ivy said. "It was nice of you to think of me. See, I'm wearing the bracelet again."

"Great," Zoey said. "So . . . how are things going?"

"Not so good. My dad still hasn't found a job."
Ivy sighed. "He's pretty depressed about it, and
Mom is working really hard all the time."

"I hope things get better soon," Zoey said.

"Yeah, me too," Ivy said. "Anyway, I better
get going. Emily texted me she's going to be here
with her mom, and I don't want to bump into
her. She'll probably try to make me buy things
with money I don't have right now." She waved
good-bye. "See you in school. By the way, the
booth looks great!"

Not long after Ivy walked away, Kate, Priti, and
Libby came back.

"What did Ivy want?" Kate asked.

"We saw her here talking to you," explained
Libby.

"Yeah, she seemed . . . almost friendly!" Priti
said.

"She *was* friendly," Zoey replied. But she'd made
a firm promise to Ivy that she'd keep her family's
situation a secret. How was she supposed to explain
why Ivy was being nice to her without giving anything away?

"What's come over her?" Libby asked.

"I . . . well, I did something nice for her, and I guess she appreciated it, so she's warming up to me or something," Zoey explained.

"*Ivy?*" Kate said. "I find it hard to believe that she's changed her spots so quickly."

"But I think she has," Zoey said. "Maybe she's just . . . getting better at seeing other people's points of view?"

"I know you've hinted that she's been behaving differently lately," Libby said. "But . . . I'm with Kate. I still think you should be really careful."

"I don't know," Priti said. "Now that I think about it, Ivy has been more friendly in class—just not when Emily is around. Maybe we should give her the benefit of the doubt."

"We should," Zoey said. "At least I think so."

"Well . . . if you think so," Libby said.

"I'll try," Kate said. "It's hard after how mean she's been. But if Zoey can do it, so can I."

The girls decided to go look around some more. Zoey didn't mind, because traffic was picking up, and she was starting to make more sales.

"Come look at these adorable bracelets!" a woman said. She reached out and pulled her daughter, who'd been hiding behind her, to the front of the booth.

It was Emily.

"Isn't this one with the ice-cream cones just the cutest thing?" Emily's mother said. "I'm going to get it for your sister. Why don't you pick one for yourself?"

Zoey held her breath, wondering what Emily would say.

"Those aren't even the real bracelets," Emily sneered. "They're copies. See, they don't have the charm showing they're the real thing." She pointed to the logo charm on one of the many bracelets she was already wearing on her wrist.

"Who cares about a logo?" Emily's mom said. "I think these are even cuter than the brand ones, and there are so many more designs to choose from. Pick one, sweetie!"

Reluctantly, Emily browsed through the tray of bracelets. She picked one with a flower design. Zoey wondered if she'd ever wear it.

"Good luck with the rest of the fair," Emily's mom said as they walked off.

Emily didn't say anything to Zoey and didn't even thank her mom for buying her the bracelet. Ivy seemed to have changed because of her dad losing his job. Zoey wondered what it would take to make Emily be nicer.

She didn't have much time to think about it because just then Ezra returned, which was fortunate since they only had a minute alone before a sudden rush of customers came to the booth. They sold a lot of the scarves, headbands, bracelets, and a few of Zoey's clothes.

"I'm really glad you decided to make the silk-screen accessories," Ezra admitted. "I can't believe so many people are going to be wearing my art!"

Zoey was having a great time with Ezra, but she couldn't help feeling the teensiest bit jealous that the silk-screen designs seemed to be outselling her own stuff. But then she remembered Daphne Shaw's comment on her blog a while back that the best designers work in teams, collaborating to create stronger work. Besides—in her heart, she *wanted* Ezra's items to sell well!

"I wonder why my friend Allie hasn't stopped by," she wondered aloud to Ezra when they had time for a breather.

"Maybe she's too busy at her booth," Ezra said.

"Maybe. But things have been a little off between us since she and Marcus broke up," Zoey explained. "Also, I'm worried that she's mad at me for doing accessories, since that's kind of her thing, not mine."

"But I thought the organizers said you needed to have more accessories to get a booth."

"They did," Zoey said. "And Allie and I made a pact not to get all competitive with each other. But still . . . She wasn't very friendly yesterday when I asked to borrow her display items."

"I think you're worrying too much!" Ezra said. "Look, here comes another customer!"

They had another small flurry of buyers. Then, as soon as things quieted down, Zoey saw Allie coming toward the booth.

"Wow, Zoey, you did such an amazing job with the booth!" she said. "So ingenious to use the twine and clothespins—and I love the ladder rack and those cool headbands."

"It was a group effort. Marcus came up with the ladder idea," Zoey said. "The twine and pins was Aunt Lulu. And Ezra's paintings are on the headbands."

"You guys make a good team," Allie said.

"Yeah," Zoey admitted, thinking about how everyone had rallied together to make her booth look great. "We do."

"Did you hear that Zoey's going to have some pieces sold at Daphne Shaw's new pop-up shop for tweens?" Ezra asked Allie. "So awesome, isn't it?"

Zoey cringed. She hadn't had a chance to tell Allie herself yet, and she was worried her friend would think she'd been keeping it from her on purpose.

Allie smiled stiffly. "It's an amazing opportunity," she said. "I read about it on the *Fashion Insider* blog. I'm really happy for you, Zoey."

Whew! So Allie already knows, Zoey thought. But she didn't seem quite as happy about it as she was saying.

"I'm really psyched, but I still don't know if I can go to the opening," Zoey said. "Dad has an away game, and Aunt Lulu's doctors want her to stick close to home because of the baby."

"That stinks!" Allie said. "We have to figure out how to get you there!"

"Well, let me know if you have any ideas," Zoey said.

"Will do. I better get back to my booth," Allie said, looking at the time on her cell. "Mom's holding down the fort, but I can't stay away too long."

"I hope she does come up with an idea," Zoey said to Ezra as Allie walked away. "Or at least I hope *someone* does."

"Yeah," Ezra agreed. "You should be there!"

Zoey and Ezra continued to chat while customers browsed the booth.

Then Allie came by, appearing to be smiling for real this time. "Guess who solved your opening night problem?" she said. "This girl! Your friend Allie Lovallo."

Ezra waved hello to Allie.

"What? *How?*" Zoey asked, hoping it was true.

"I talked to my mom, and we realized that the Daphne Shaw opening is the same weekend Mom and I are planning to go to New York City to look at a fashion design school I'm thinking of applying to for college," Allie explained. "Mom said that we could give you a ride, and she'd be your chaperone at the opening, if Daphne doesn't mind putting us on the guest list and if your dad's okay with it."

"I'm sure she wouldn't mind," Zoey said. "But I'll e-mail her right now to ask—and I'll call Dad!"

Her father agreed with the condition that he wanted to speak to Allie's mom about the details. Before the gift fair closed, Daphne had replied to Zoey's e-mail saying that she'd be happy to put Allie and her mom on the guest list if it meant that Zoey could be there.

"My problem is solved!" Zoey said, hugging Ezra. "I'm going to the opening!"

"Roll out the red carpet." Ezra laughed. "Sew Zoey's in the house!"

Zoey chuckled. "Now comes the hard part," Zoey said. "Figuring out what to *wear!*"

CHAPTER 11

Pop-Up Shop Bop

It's been nonstop sewing! As soon as I finished making the clothes for the gift fair, I had to start making the clothes for the next exciting event: Daphne Shaw's pop-up shop for her tween clothing line! Daphne's selected two of my pieces to display in the shop. It's meant I've been superbusy and have barely had any time to spend with my friends (sorry, Priti, Kate, Libby . . . and everyone else!), but I'm sure it will be worth it! And I've been making this dress using—guess what?—leftover screen-printed fabric with my friend's painting. It was his idea, and I'm really excited to wear it.

I'm driving up with Allie and her mom—we're going to tour the City Fashion Institute in the morning and then attend the opening that evening. I can't wait! I hope my dress is fancy enough. Allie said she thinks it will rock the red carpet. I'll let you know!

"I can't believe we're here!" Zoey exclaimed in the car with Allie and her mom as they crossed the bridge and viewed the New York City skyline.

The weeks between the gift fair and the opening had been really hard work—making all the pieces Daphne ordered for the pop-up shop and keeping up with her schoolwork at the same time. But it was worth it, because tonight she'd see her clothes being sold in a real department store next to her mentor's!

"First, we'll go to the fashion institute for the tour, then check in at the hotel," Mrs. Lovallo said.

"Are you excited to look at the school?" Zoey asked Allie.

"We looked at a few liberal arts colleges over the summer, but this is my first fashion design school. Dad thinks I should get a liberal arts education before I focus on fashion." Allie sighed. "You know, 'just in case.'"

"My dad is the same way," Zoey said. "But my aunt Lulu said that I should follow my dream and do what I really feel passionate about. It seems to have worked for her!"

The fashion design school seemed like heaven on Earth to Zoey as they toured it. She couldn't believe that there was a place where she could go to school to learn all the ins and outs of making and designing clothes and running a fashion business.

There were whole rooms filled with sewing machines and dress forms, and a fashion library where students could research the history of design.

"I want to apply here when I have to think about

going to college!" Zoey exclaimed. "I wish I could go now instead of having to wait."

"Yeah, it's pretty exciting to think about being able to spend more time on learning about the things I'm *really* interested in," Allie agreed.

"Now that we're done here, let's check in to the hotel," Mrs. Lovallo said. "I've got a surprise for you both before the opening tonight."

After they'd put their bags in the hotel room and hung up their dresses for the opening, Mrs. Lovallo took the girls down the street to a beauty salon.

"I booked us all appointments to get our hair and nails done," she said. "It's not every day a girl gets to walk the red carpet!"

"Thank you!" Zoey said.

Allie and Zoey helped each other pick out polish colors for their nails, and they were seated at adjacent manicurists while Mrs. Lovallo got her hair done.

"Zoey," Allie asked hesitantly. "Are you mad at me?"

"No," Zoey said, surprised at the question.

"Are you *sure*?" Allie persisted.

"Well . . . I guess I'm upset that your relationship with Marcus ended the way it did, but you can't force yourself to like my brother if you like someone else," Zoey said. "I just wish you'd been more honest with him, is all."

"So . . . why didn't you visit my booth at the gift fair?" Allie asked.

"What? I thought you were avoiding *me*!" Zoey said. "And things got so busy."

"I was busy, too," Allie said. "But I finally went to your booth because I thought you were mad at me for not lending you display materials. And we'd promised we wouldn't let things get weird."

"I *was* a little mad about that," Zoey admitted. "I was desperate, and it seemed like you didn't want to help that much."

"I'm sorry," Allie said. "It's just that I had a plan for how I was going to display my stuff, and I didn't know what I'd do if I gave you more. I don't have Marcus and Aunt Lulu to come up with the great creative solutions you ended up doing."

"But you're more creative than most people I know!" Zoey protested. "I still don't understand why you wouldn't help a friend. Are you sure there wasn't something else going on?"

Allie was silent for a moment, and then she said, "You're right. I have a confession to make. When I read on *Fashion Insider* that you were going to have two pieces in Daphne Shaw's pop-up store, I got jealous. *Really* jealous. I don't know what came over me at the gift fair, but I realized later that I kind of didn't want to share my display things because I felt like you already had so much going for you and it wasn't fair. I feel horrible about it now—like, I'm the worst friend ever. Can you forgive me?"

Zoey was shocked at first, but then she remembered how she started to feel jealous that Ezra's silk-screen items were selling better than her stuff. And that wasn't nearly as big of a deal as having two of her pieces in Daphne Shaw's pop-up store.

"I understand," Zoey said. "I'm glad you told me the truth."

"I've been feeling really bad about it. And then the gift fair didn't go as well for me this year as it did last year, which just made me feel worse," Allie confessed. "How did it go for you?"

"Pretty well," Zoey said. "But I sold more of the scarves and headbands with Ezra's silk-screened paintings than I did of my own clothing designs. I guess they were right about clothes not selling so well at the gift fair."

"Those scarves were cool," Allie said. "But what I really want to know is . . . do you hate me now that I told you all that?"

"Of course not!" Zoey said. "We all have our moments. If it wasn't for you and your mom, I wouldn't be going to the opening at all, and I'm really glad you're coming with me."

"Me too," Allie said. "I can't wait. You know what, though—I think my mom's even more excited than I am!"

Daphne sent a car to pick them up at the hotel and bring them to the department store for the opening.

"I can't believe it's really the night of the opening," Zoey said. "I've been so busy sewing the pieces, I haven't had that much time to get excited."

"But you're excited now, I hope?" Mrs. Lovallo asked.

"Yes!" Zoey exclaimed. "I've got butterflies!"

As soon as they walked into the store, Daphne's assistant Jessie, who Zoey remembered from her visit to the designer's studio, took them over to the press area, where there was a red velvet carpet, a gaggle of photographers, and a few reporters and cameramen from TV stations.

Zoey couldn't believe this was real. She closed her eyes and opened them again to make sure everything was still there. She noticed her hands were shaking, but she didn't know if she was more nervous or more excited.

Allie brought her back to reality. "I never realized that the red carpet was just a fake wall with a bit of carpet in front," Allie whispered. "Crazy, right?"

"Me neither," Zoey said. "I thought it was a really long red carpet!"

Just then Daphne slipped through the crowd and surprised Zoey. "You made it!" Daphne said, giving Zoey a big hug. She turned to Allie and Mrs. Lovallo. "And you must be Zoey's wonderful friend Allie, and I take it you're Mrs. Lovallo? Great to meet you both."

Allie lit up when Daphne called her "wonderful friend," and Zoey hoped it made up for any jealousy she might have felt earlier.

Daphne walked them on to the red carpet platform, and they posed in front of the background wall, which had the new Daphne Shaw tween logo all over it.

"Over here!" one photographer after another shouted, and Zoey, Allie, Mrs. Lovallo—and Daphne, of course—kept smiling and looking toward the cameras.

"My face hurts from smiling," Zoey said as they walked off the carpet.

"I know how you feel," Daphne said. "I've been in so many photos, I think my jaw is locked in the smile position. Now, go enjoy yourself—and make sure to try the miniquiches. They're excellent!"

The pop-up store was a huge, white circular platform at the very center of the department store's main floor.

"Very classy," Mrs. Lovallo said.

"Look, Zoey! There you are!" Allie exclaimed.

Sure enough, there was a clothing rack with her

skirt and top hung in a variety of sizes she'd just recently sent to Daphne. She couldn't believe the clothes she'd made in her house not long ago were now in a real department store, with official-looking price tags attached and bar codes and everything. Above the clothes was a sign that said DESIGNS BY SEW ZOEY alongside a photo of Zoey and a small blurb that explained how Zoey and her blog had helped inspire Daphne's tween collection.

"Let me take a picture of you girls next to Zoey's clothing rack for Mr. Webber," Mrs. Lovallo said.

Allie and Zoey took one serious photo, and then they goofed around and pointed at the picture of Zoey.

"I thought there were going to be just old people here, but there are a bunch of other kids," Allie said.

"It's the launch of a tween line, honey," Mrs. Lovallo said. "Ms. Shaw probably wanted to invite some fashion-forward customers who might spread the word."

"I'm glad there are other kids here," Zoey said. "It makes it less intimidating than if it were all grown-ups."

"Zoey!" Ceci Miller, who had been a fellow judge on *Fashion Showdown*, came over with one of the other judges, Christophe LeFrak. She gave Zoey air-kisses. "Congratulations!"

"Yes, it is exciting that our young judge inspired Daphne's new line," Christophe said. *"Félicitations, ma petite."*

Zoey introduced them to Allie and her mom, and they were chatting when Oscar Bradesco, the host of *Fashion Showdown*, came to say hello.

Both Lovallos seemed totally starstruck to meet him. When he walked away, after kissing Mrs. Lovallo's hand, Mrs. Lovallo said, "I can't believe I just got air-kissed by someone I've seen on TV!"

Zoey's phone buzzed. It was a text from Ezra.

How's it going?

AMAZING! she texted back. **Can't wait to tell you all about it!**

That night, when they were back at the hotel, Dad called to ask Zoey about her big night. She told him the great news: Her clothes were back-ordered in a few sizes already! They had to refill the rack from the stockroom, and were going to arrange for a vendor to manufacture the clothes to keep up with demand!

"I'm really proud of you," he told Zoey after she'd given him a rundown of the evening's festivities. "I wish I could have been there."

"I know," Zoey said. "I wish you could have been here too."

"Listen, Zo . . . I've got some news. The Mystery Lady and I decided it's time for you all to meet."

"Wow!" Zoey said, stunned by the news. "When?"

"I invited her for dinner tomorrow night, after you get back from the city," Dad said. "She's really looking forward to it."

"So am I," Zoey said.

But after she hung up, she wasn't so sure. If Dad decided they should meet the Mystery Lady, things must be getting superserious. Zoey wasn't sure she was ready for that. First, Aunt Lulu was about to have a baby, and now Dad was getting serious with a woman she hadn't even met?

She dialed Marcus's cell.

"Hey, Zo, how was the shindig?" Marcus asked.

"It was great, but . . . did Dad tell you?"

"About meeting the Mystery Lady? Yeah. *Finally!*"

"I'm not sure I want to meet her," Zoey confessed.

"What! Why not?" Marcus exclaimed. "We've been nagging him to introduce us for months!"

"I know . . . but do you think this means they're going to get married?" Zoey asked. "I don't know if I'm ready for a stepmother I've never met."

"First of all, you're going to meet her. At dinner tomorrow," Marcus said. "And as for the stepmother thing . . . I know what you mean, but I think we have to trust Dad. I mean, he picked Mom, right?"

Zoey hadn't thought of it that way, but once she did, she felt better. At least kind of better. So much was changing. She just hoped the Mystery Lady was all she was cracked up to be.

CHAPTER 12

What a Gift!

Well, it's back to regular life as a middle schooler after a weekend of the fancy New York City fashion world! Sometimes I can't believe this is my life—it's like I won some lottery or some huge gift just by doing what I love—and then I get a pop quiz and come back to Earth. I can see the book title now: *From Pop Quiz to Pop-Up Shop: The Sew Zoey Story*. Ha-ha. Anyway, I was so busy I didn't even have time to do a sketch for today's post. Instead, check out a sketch of those scarves and headbands I made with my friend's paintings for the gift fair. This time, I got his permission to use the images—lesson learned—and I hope you'll think they're as cool as I do! Also, these are the two pieces for sale in Daphne's shop—an origami shirt and flared skirt, courtesy of yours truly.

And now for more about last night. It was an *amazing* time: Mrs. Lovallo treated us to mani-pedis and blowouts, which meant my hair was perfect all night. How nice was that?! The event itself was less intimidating than I thought it would be, because there were other kids my age there—and I got to see Christophe LeFrak and Ceci Miller, my fellow judges from *Fashion Showdown*, as well as Oscar Bradesco, who hosted when I was a judge. I just missed meeting Daphne Shaw on that occasion— but now I have my clothes in her pop-up shop! It goes to show that you never know how one thing can lead to another. . . .

When Zoey got back to Mapleton on Sunday afternoon, she got a phone call from Ezra, who sounded superexcited.

"Guess what! Your friend Jan bought one of my paintings for her store!" he said. "I've never sold a painting before. . . . I'm officially a working artist!"

"Awesome!" Zoey said. "Looks like Marcus's postcards worked."

"Thanks again for doing the scarves and headbands," Ezra said. "I know I kind of freaked out at first, but I'm really glad you did it. We did pretty well with them, didn't we?"

"Yeah—I was nervous about not making enough to cover the cost of the booth, but thanks to your accessories, it wasn't a problem," Zoey said. "That reminds me, I have to give you your share of the profits."

"Do you want to get together after school this week? I want to hear all about the opening, too!" Ezra said.

They arranged to get together on Wednesday, and Zoey hung up just as Dad called, asking her to come downstairs and help him. He was busy preparing for dinner with the Mystery Lady, and Zoey could tell he was nervous by the way he wanted everything to be just so.

"What tablecloth should I use?" he asked, holding up two different ones.

"We haven't used a tablecloth since . . . I can't remember when," Zoey said. "But if I had to choose, I'd say that one." She pointed to the cotton one with embroidered flowers.

"Can you and Marcus set the table and make it look nice?" Dad asked. "Make sure you use cloth napkins and not paper ones."

Marcus and Zoey exchanged glances.

"Sure, Dad," Zoey said. "Real napkins it is."

"Uh, Dad?" Marcus said. "It's just dinner, not a presidential banquet."

"You might just be right," Dad said, "but I really want tonight to go well."

"Chill, Dad," Zoey said. "It'll be fine."

"It's actually kind of cute how nervous he is, isn't it, Zo?" Marcus said.

Dad laughed.

"Go ahead and tease," he warned. "I'll remember

this when you both are nervous about introducing *your* significant others to *me!*"

When the doorbell rang at six o'clock, Dad jumped up to answer the door before Zoey and Marcus could even think about it. They waited in the kitchen, hearing muffled voices as Dad greeted his guest.

"What's taking them so long?" Marcus whispered to Zoey when they hadn't come into the kitchen after a few minutes.

"Do you think she changed her mind about meeting us at the last minute?" Zoey whispered back.

"No way," Marcus replied in a low voice. "We've waited too long."

He called out into the hallway, "Hey, Dad? Are you coming? We don't want dinner to get overcooked!"

"Be right there," Dad called back.

Zoey's heart started beating faster in anticipation of seeing the woman who might, one day, maybe, become her stepmother.

Dad walked back into the kitchen. Behind him was . . . *Ms. Austen?*

Zoey was confused. Why was her principal visiting her house at dinnertime on Sunday? She couldn't think of anything she'd done wrong at all, much less something that would be bad enough to require a home visit from the head of the school.

Zoey was in the middle of admiring Ms. Austen's flouncy dress—which was tailored and tasteful but less buttoned-up than her usual attire as school principal—when suddenly it dawned on her that something big was happening. "Wait . . . *Ms. Austen* is the Mystery Lady?" she blurted out.

"I am," Ms. Austen said, smiling as Dad put his arm across her shoulders. "I hope you both understand now why your dad and I felt like it was best we kept things discreet until we had a better idea of where this was going."

Zoey couldn't have been more surprised. But then she thought back to the day when her dad and Ms. Austen shared an animated and very smiley conversation in the parking lot at school when Dad was waiting for her . . . and how the person who picked the baby present for Aunt Lulu's shower had such great taste . . . and how Dad had a date at the art museum . . . and suddenly the pieces fell into place.

"It *does* make more sense," Zoey admitted.

"Yeah, I can see how it would be awkward for you—and for Zoey!" Marcus said. "But I've only heard great things about you, Ms. Austen, for the record."

Ms. Austen smiled warmly. "Likewise, Marcus. And you can call me Essie, if you want."

Marcus shrugged, and Zoey stepped in. "Can we stick with 'Ms. Austen' for now?" Zoey asked. "This is already kind of weird, and I think it'll be weirder to call you by your first name!"

"Whatever works for you," Ms. Austen said kindly.

Zoey remembered when she'd first seen that name way back when she'd first learned about the change in the uniform policy in a letter from her school's new principal, Ms. Esther Austen. She never would have guessed that this one person could change so much in her own life in a short time, and maybe for the better.

As they ate dinner and she watched Ms. Austen

and Dad smiling at each other, Zoey wondered if her school principal—who apparently went by the name "Essie"—was going to be her new stepmom.

It wouldn't be so bad, Zoey thought. She loved Ms. Austen, and they had a lot in common—they both loved fashion and, it seemed, her dad. And she hadn't seen her dad this happy in as long as she could remember.

But how weird would it be to have your step-mom as a principal? Especially as *your* principal? Zoey had no idea how that would work—but if Ms. Austen made Dad this happy, Zoey was going to try really hard to make sure it did! So much was changing with Dad and the now not-so-Mystery Lady and Aunt Lulu's baby on the way. Zoey had no idea what her family was going to look like in the future, but of one thing she could be certain: They would all be *very* well dressed!

Don't be fashionably late!
Look out for the next book
in the Sew Zoey series:

CUT
FROM THE
same
CLOTH